Praise for DEATH AT A COUNTRY MANSION

"Sharper than a pair of scissors, more fun than a manicure, Daisy Thorne is no ordinary hairdresser and when her best friend's mother is murdered, she combs through clues looking for the killer. *Death at a Country Mansion* has more twists than a French braid."—**Sherry Harris**, author of the Sarah Winston Garage Sale mysteries and the Chloe Jackson Sea Glass Saloon mysteries

"*Death at a Country Mansion* is a fun romp through the British countryside, with Daisy Thorne, hairdresser, leading a colorful cast of characters to solve the murder of her dear friend Floria's famous mother. Daisy is smart, savvy, and full of spirit. This book has a delightful puzzle with a satisfying ending. Everyone who loves a manor house mystery will love this one."—**Nancy Coco**, author of the Candy-Coated mystery series

"Multiple suspects, myriad motives, and a missing Modigliani add up to murder at the manor. Louise Rose Innes is constantly twisting the story just as we, the reader, believe we've figured out the murderer. If you enjoy British manor houses, a touch of budding romance, and a good mystery (like I do), I highly recommend *Death at a Country Mansion*."—**Vikki Walton**, bestselling author of the Backyard Farming mystery series and the Taylor Texas mystery series

Death at a Country Mansion

—•A Daisy Thorne Mystery•—

LOUISE R. INNES

KENSINGTON BOOKS
KENSINGTON PUBLISHING CORP.
www.kensingtonbooks.com

KENSINGTON BOOKS are published by

Kensington Publishing Corp.
119 West 40th Street
New York, NY 10018

All Kensington titles, imprints, and distributed lines are available at special
quantity discounts for bulk purchases for sales promotion, premiums,
fund-raising, educational, or institutional use.

Special book excerpts or customized printings can also be created to fit
specific needs. For details, write or phone the office of the Kensington
Sales Manager: Attn.: Sales Department. Kensington Publishing Corp.,
119 West 40th Street, New York, NY 10018. Phone: 1-800-221-2647.

Kensington and the K logo Reg. U.S. Pat. & TM Off.

First Printing: December 2020
ISBN-13: 978-1-4967-2980-4
ISBN-10: 1-4967-2980-3

ISBN-13: 978-1-4967-2981-1 (eBook)
ISBN-10: 1-4967-2981-1 (eBook)

10 9 8 7 6 5 4 3 2 1

Printed in the United States of America

For Karen

Chapter One

The ice in her glass tinkled provocatively as the scotch hit it. Another marriage in tatters. Her fourth, in fact. Serena shook her head and took a big gulp, feeling the whiskey encase her in a golden glow as it went down. Bastard. How could Collin do this to her? With an air hostess, of all people. What the hell was he thinking?

She'd arrived home earlier that afternoon to find her husband packing. The lunch meeting with her solicitor had finished earlier than expected; otherwise she'd never have caught him.

"I'm leaving you, Serena." He tossed shorts and T-shirts into his suitcase, then fumbled in his dresser for the sunscreen. "I wanted to avoid a confrontation, but you're here, so you may as well hear it from me. You're a drunk. You've made my life intolerable. I've had it with your bitching and sniping, not to mention your blatant attempts to seduce every red-blooded man who walks through the door. Christ, you're an embarrassment."

She'd been so stunned; she hadn't known how to respond. Yes, her drinking had gotten out of hand lately, and she had tried to chat up that handsome, young musician at the summer party, but that was Collin's fault for ignoring her. What did he expect her to do? He certainly didn't touch her anymore.

He continued, "I've met someone, someone who appreciates me. We're going to the house in the Bahamas. My solicitor will be in touch." Collin hauled the heavy suitcase onto the landing. It was the beige one, the same one he'd had on their honeymoon.

Feeling a surge of rage, she'd stumbled after him. "What do you mean you've met someone? Who?"

"None of your business."

"What do you mean it's none of my business? You're my husband, for Christ's sake. Who is she?" She was screeching now, a horrid, high-pitched sound tinged with desperation.

"If you must know, her name is Bernadette, and she's an air hostess. We met on my last trip to Paris."

Serena stared at him. This couldn't be happening. "How dare you walk out on me! And that's my house in the Bahamas. I bought it and I forbid you to use it as a sordid shag pad." Her voice rose hysterically, as it often did when she'd been drinking, and she'd had a bottle of sauvignon blanc with lunch.

He turned to face her, his voice unusually calm. Normally, they'd both be screaming at each other by now. "That's rich, coming from you. And for your information, we put the Nassau house in my name, remember? For tax purposes. It's mine now." He smirked and picked up the suitcase to carry it downstairs.

The grand staircase was Serena's favorite feature in the stately old mansion, and the main reason she'd bought it almost three decades before. It seemed like a lifetime. She adored the glorious mahogany balustrade with spiral spindles that Violeta, the housekeeper, kept polished to a high shine, and the soft lilac carpeting with gold strips. It reminded her of elegant Venetian palaces and old-fashioned grandeur. She'd once performed for a select group of guests, standing at the top of the grand staircase. The rapture on their faces as she sung Puccini's "O Mio Babbino Caro" had made her heart soar.

Serena floundered after him, coming to an unsteady halt on the landing. "Please, Collin, don't do this. Let's talk about it."

He'd glanced up, but instead of looking at her, his gaze rose to the portrait of the woman she'd once been, which hung above her head. That's when she knew it was truly over. He couldn't even look at her anymore. She turned up her face to the painting, grasping the balustrade so as not to lose her balance. It had been commissioned at the height of her fame, and the beautiful, serene expression on her face made her heart twist every time she saw it. She'd been so happy then. Life had been magical. Her records were selling, her concerts were sold out, everyone wanted a piece of her. How had it all gone so wrong?

"I didn't want it to end like this, you know." Collin's face softened momentarily. "But you left me no choice. Living with you has become . . . impossible."

At that point, she'd fallen to her knees, tears streaming down her face.

"I hope you find some peace, Serena."

And he walked out of the house, pulling his suitcase behind him.

Serena hung her head and sobbed, great rasping sounds that resonated from the depths of her soul. The hand holding the tumbler drooped, spilling the drink on the Persian rug. She didn't care. How had her life come to this?

Age was a bitch. Once she'd hit fifty, her voice had gone downhill, no doubt helped along by the booze and the screaming matches with her husband. But without her singing, she was nothing, just an empty shell, and no matter how much she drank or how many lovers she took, she couldn't fill the void. Her laser-sharp soprano voice, which had once captivated the masses and enthralled royalty, was no more. She'd lost that iridescent quality that allowed her to scale the fearsome heights of the most physically demanding music. She poured another drink, then another. Eventually, the sought-after haze descended and her head lolled back onto the headrest of the chaise longue.

Serena woke with a start in the middle of the night and looked around in a panic. Where was she? Oh, yeah. She was still on the chaise longue, fully clothed.

What was that noise that had woken her? Was it the front door? She listened, holding her breath. The room swam in front of her eyes and her tongue was parched. A wave of nausea hit her and she bent over, fearing she might be sick. God, she'd polished off most of the scotch. That was heavy, even for her. There was a loud creak on the staircase. She recognized it. The loose board before the landing.

Someone was in the house.

She glanced around for a weapon, but all she could find was the empty whiskey bottle on the side table. Grabbing it by the neck, she stumbled toward the door. Her heart pounded as she peered onto the landing.

Relief flooded her body. "Oh, thank God, it's you. You almost gave me a heart attack."

She dropped her arm carrying the bottle, just as the intruder raised his.

Serena screamed as she realized what was happening. Then came the hammer blow. Her head exploded in pain and she fell to her knees. The room spun, she was so dizzy.

"Why?" She reached out, trying to grab something, anything to stabilize herself. Her hand folded around the balustrade.

The intruder lifted her to her feet, and for a moment she thought it might be okay, but then he bent her over the railing. Her hand tightened its grip as she flopped forward.

"No, please . . ."

The intruder pried her fingers loose. It wasn't hard; she had no strength left. Then she felt herself falling. It was a strange sensation, and for a fleeting moment she felt weightless and free. Then the air was knocked out of her and darkness descended.

Chapter Two

Daisy was on her hands and knees weeding the garden when her mobile phone rang. It was the beginning of summer, and before she could plant the multitude of colorful potted geraniums she'd bought from the garden center, she first had to purge the beds of weeds. The pesky invaders seemed to have taken root in the spring, thanks to the unseasonably warm weather, and had multiplied at a speed to rival that of a time-lapse camera. The upbeat ringtone interrupted the audio lecture she was listening to on her iPad on the emotions of violent offenses, part of the forensic psychology degree she was studying via correspondence. She pulled off a well-used gardening glove to answer it.

"Hi, Flo."

"Daisy?" There was a loud sniff. "Oh, Daisy . . . " Her best friend's voice wobbled, and Daisy could hear she'd been crying. It wasn't like Floria to get upset. She was normally such a positive, bubbly person. Something awful must have happened to reduce her to tears.

"Floria, what's wrong?"

"It's Mother. She–she's dead." The voice cracked.

"What?" Daisy thought she'd misheard. The audio recording was saying: *In violent crime, feelings such as humiliation, righteousness, arrogance, ridicule, cynicism, defilement and vengeance give the offender the feeling that he or she has a moral right to attack.* Daisy reached for her iPad and pressed Stop.

Floria's voice was hollow. "Mother's dead. She had an accident. Oh, Daisy, please, will you come to the house?"

"Of course. I'll meet you there."

Daisy didn't need an explanation as to which house. Floria's mother, Dame Serena Levanté, the famous opera singer—who had graced the pages of almost all of the tabloids at some point over the last twenty years—lived at Brompton Court, a stately home that lay halfway between Daisy's small village of Edgemead and the slightly larger town of Esher in Surrey.

Heart pounding, she dashed inside and changed out of her dirty gardening clothes into fresh jeans and a blouse, only pausing to wash her hands and run a comb through her blond hair, which currently looked like it could rival the bird's nest in the elm tree outside. What on earth had happened?

Serena dead? Floria had mentioned an accident. Had she had a car crash? Perhaps she'd been driving under the influence. It wouldn't be the first time.

Daisy's mind was racing as she jumped into her trusty Honda and reversed quickly out of the gravel driveway, nearly backing into Mr. Henderson's flower delivery van, trundling up the road. He swerved onto the grassy verge to avoid her, then put his hand on the horn.

"Sorry, Frank!" she yelled out of the window as she sped off in the direction of Brompton Court.

* * *

Floria Levanté was a socialite and reformed wild child, as well as being one of Daisy's closest friends. She still remembered how they'd first met. It was a funny story, and one they took great pleasure in reminiscing over, especially after a few drinks at the Fox and Hound, the local pub. It had been Ladies Day at the prestigious Ascot horse races about five years before. Floria had bounced into the salon to have her hair done and Daisy had tended to her. The moment they'd got chatting, Daisy had known Floria was a kindred spirit. She'd brought out the prosecco, and by the time Floria's hair was done in a stylish updo and her Piers Atkinson attention-grabbing headpiece fixed stoutly into place, they were firm friends. She recalled giggling over the horses' names on the race sheet Floria was studying.

"He was renamed Bunny Killer because he trampled over a bunny in his first race," Floria explained, trying to keep a straight face. "I swear, it's true. I know the trainer."

"Look at this one," said Daisy. "He's called Badly. Can you imagine the commentator? 'Here we have John Smith riding Badly.'" They went off into peals of laughter.

"Broomstick, now that's a good name," said Daisy. "Perhaps you should go for that one."

"Sounds like the perfect horse for my mother," remarked Floria, setting Daisy off again. Dame Serena was known to be a veritable witch at times, but that fact was carefully kept out of the papers, thanks to the Herculean efforts of her long-suffering publicity agent.

Floria convinced Daisy to join her and her friends at the races. At first she'd refused, not wanting to intrude, but thanks to the prosecco and Floria's persuasive charm, she relented. So, after a manic dash home so Daisy could change, they'd caught a cab to Ascot. What Daisy hadn't known at the time was that Floria ran with a very posh set of friends. All ex-public school girls who came from wealthy, Surrey middle-class families and worked part-time in Mayfair at art galleries, shopped in New Bond Street, and had memberships to private clubs. The men were university educated, with burgeoning careers in finance or banking in the City. Not the kind of crowd Daisy was used to hanging out with. However, once she got to know them, Daisy fitted right in. Her natural exuberance and easy sense of humor endeared her to all Floria's friends. The Pimms flowed, the betting commenced, and by the end of a very long, boozy day, Daisy knew she'd made a friend for life.

Daisy raced up the extensive driveway to Brompton Court, her tires crunching and skidding on the gravel. The private lane wound through acres of beautifully landscaped gardens, tended to by the ever-diligent Pepe, and opened into a gravel car park in front of the house. The midmorning sun shone directly onto the stone Palladian mansion, bathing it in a soft, golden hue. Usually, Daisy paused to admire the shimmering façade which never ceased to take her breath away, but today she was distracted by the flashing lights of the ambulance and several police cars outside.

Floria was deep in conversation with a tall, broad-shouldered man holding a notepad. A plainclothed detective, no doubt. Daisy was surprised by his casual attire: dark-blue jeans and a beige T-shirt straining across the shoulders as if complaining about the detective's bulk.

He really needed a bigger size. It was a far cry from the formal suit and tie her grandfather used to wear when he was in the CID, but then, that was twenty years ago, and it was the weekend. His expression was serious, bordering on annoyed, as if he didn't appreciate being called out on a beautiful Sunday morning at the beginning of summer. He glanced up as Daisy approached.

Floria threw herself into her friend's arms. "Oh, Daisy. Can you believe it? Mother's dead."

Daisy hugged her, worried by how tightly Floria clung to her. After she'd disentangled herself, she stretched out an arm toward the officer. "Hello, I'm Daisy Thorne."

The detective gave a curt nod and returned the handshake. It was firm and brief. A no-nonsense handshake like his demeanor. "DI Paul McGuinness, Surrey CID. Are you related to Miss Levanté?"

"No, I'm her best friend."

He glanced from one to the other, frown lines on his brow. He was sizing them up. Most people did when they went out together. Similar in looks, they both had pale blond hair and blue eyes, but while Daisy was tall and lanky, Floria was of average height and curvy. She'd made an excellent Marilyn Monroe at last year's Hollywood-themed ball. Daisy had gone as Uma Thurman in *Kill Bill*, complete with yellow jumpsuit.

Daisy shot him a coquettish smile, but it didn't have the desired effect. It seemed the gruff detective was immune to her charms or deliberately ignoring them. He returned an icy stare. "I'm sorry, Miss Thorne, but this is an active crime scene and you can't be here."

Floria gripped her friend's hand. Daisy gave it a re-assuring squeeze. There was no way she was leaving.

Floria needed her as never before, and it would take more than the detective's arctic stare and terse words to intimidate her.

"I'm needed for moral support, Detective Inspector," said Daisy firmly. "Can't you see Floria is distraught?"

Her friend's lip quivered obligingly. "I don't have anyone else to call. My father lives in France and I have no siblings. Please, let her stay?"

The detective inspector stared at them for a moment, then obviously decided to let it slide. He changed tack, turning his attention back to the investigation. "Where is Dame Serena Levanté's husband?"

Daisy pursed her lips. "Collin? I don't know. Isn't he here?"

Floria welled up. "I haven't seen him. Every time I close my eyes I see Mother lying at the foot of the stairs." She turned to Daisy. "Oh, Daisy, it was too terrible. I saw her body . . . lying there . . . staring up at the ceiling. . . . Her eyes were still open." A shudder ran through her voluptuous frame.

Daisy reached out and hugged her again, holding her close while DI McGuinness made a note in his little black book. "We'll have to trace him. Do you have his mobile phone number?"

Floria sniffed. "It's in my phone."

When she didn't move, the detective prodded, "Would you mind getting it for me?"

Daisy stepped back as Floria pulled out the device from her back pocket and looked up the number. DI McGuinness scribbled it onto a page, which he tore off, then he beckoned to a young sergeant standing nearby, who immediately came over. He had large, square shoulders and a flat, earnest face. Daisy guessed ex-military.

"Buckley, I need you to trace Collin Harrison, Dame Levanté's husband." He handed the sergeant the slip of paper. "Do it now."

It wouldn't hurt for him to say 'please' occasionally, Daisy thought.

"Yes, sir." The sergeant pulled out his phone and walked away from the group to make a call.

Just then, Violeta, the Levantés' elderly housekeeper, shuffled over. Daisy was shocked by how pale the Italian woman looked. Reaching out, the housekeeper clutched Floria and Daisy's hands in both of hers. She was trembling, the vibrations flowing through her worn fingers into Daisy's. "I find her this morning. Oh, dio mio! Is too terrible. I can't believe she gone." In her distress, her English had faltered.

"You're shaking, Violeta." Daisy was concerned. It was clear the woman was suffering from shock. Her eyes were wide and had a wild, unfocused look in them like she wanted desperately to unsee something but couldn't. "Let's get you inside."

She put an arm around the housekeeper. The detective opened his mouth, but before he could get a word out, Daisy interjected, "We'll be in the kitchen if you need us. Everyone's nerves are shattered. I think a strong cup of tea is in order."

DI McGuinness, knowing when he was defeated, closed his mouth. Daisy shepherded everyone around the side of the house to the kitchen entrance, so they wouldn't have to walk through the main hall, where forensic technicians were processing the crime scene. She put on the kettle and brought out Violeta's favorite tea set, the one with little lemons painted on the cups and saucers. The housekeeper had once told them she'd bought it on the island of Capri and it reminded her of her native Italy.

Once seated around the rustic kitchen table, cups of sweet tea in front of them, Daisy asked gently, "Tell us what happened, Violeta?"

The Italian woman raised her eyes to the heavens and shook her head. She seemed somewhat calmer now, thanks to the tea, the initial shock having worn off.

"I popped in to get my statins, which I keep in the kitchen cupboard so I don't forget to take them. Sunday's my day off, so I not normally here. Anyway, I took one and was about to leave when I think the house is very quiet. There's usually some music playing." She glanced at Floria, "You know what she's like, loud opera all hours of the day and night. So, I go to check, and that's when I find her lying at the bottom of the stairs, all bent and buckled like a rag doll." The housekeeper closed her eyes as if in prayer. "I never forget the look on her face. Her eyes were open, but she looked terrified, like she seen a ghost."

"What do you think happened?"

"It looked like she fell. I found an empty whiskey bottle on the upstairs landing." She bit her lip and frowned. "She was fully dressed too, in the same clothes as yesterday. She did not go to bed."

Probably passed out fully clothed, Daisy surmised. Floria had told her that Dame Serena's drinking had become so bad of late that the famous opera singer hardly ever left the house.

Floria clutched the hand of the woman who'd practically raised her. "It's okay, Violeta. The drink was bound to get her eventually, although I must admit, I didn't see this coming. I thought she'd end up in a rehab center or wrap her Mercedes around a tree, not topple headfirst over the balustrade of her own home."

"It's hard to take in." Daisy turned to her friend, thinking she looked rather pale. "You can stay with me for a couple of days, Floria, if you like, just until the shock wears off."

Relief flashed across Floria's face. "Thanks, that would be great. I don't want to be alone right now. Not after this. Mother and I were never close, as you know, but seeing her like that, so lifeless . . . " She let her sentence hang.

"It's been a terrible shock for everyone," Daisy murmured. From what Floria had let slip over the years, parenting hadn't been Serena's strong point. Floria had been raised by an endless troupe of nannies and au pairs, until she'd been old enough to be shipped off to boarding school, and even then, it hadn't been weekly boarding but full-time boarding, with Floria only allowed home for the holidays. From what Daisy could make out, most of those holidays were spent either with friends or Violeta and Pepe, who lived in the gatehouse on the property. Why the woman had ever had a child, she couldn't fathom.

"I wonder where Collin is?" Floria wrapped her hands around her teacup. In light of what had transpired, Serena's fourth husband was conspicuously absent.

"He gone," whispered Violeta.

Both Daisy and Floria stared at her in surprise.

"What do you mean, gone?" Floria carefully put down her cup. "Like gone for the day, or gone permanently?"

"What do you know, Violeta?" asked Daisy slowly.

Violeta shrugged in a way only Italians can. "He left her to run away with his lover. I think he finally had enough."

"His lover? You mean Collin was having an affair?" Floria frowned.

It was the first Daisy had heard of it too. Collin had kept that one awfully quiet.

"With whom?" demanded Floria.

The housekeeper shook her head, like she didn't know where to start.

"Why don't you start from the beginning?" Daisy suggested in a calm voice. "What happened yesterday?"

Violeta leaned against the hard wooden back of the chair as if trying to absorb some support from it. She closed her eyes briefly, gathering her thoughts. "Serena had gone to meet her solicitor, your nice friend, Mr. Edwards, but she'd come home early. I wasn't expecting her till much later. She'd been drinking. I could see it in her face. Her cheeks were pink and her eyes had that strange look in them." She glanced at Floria, who knew that look well. She'd been the brunt of it many times over the years. Unfortunately, so did Daisy. "Glazed and unfocused" would have been a better way of describing it.

Violeta continued. "Collin was upstairs packing. He asked me to iron some shirts to take away with him. I think he wanted to leave before *she* got home." She shrugged again. "But his plan didn't work. Serena came home and asked him where he was going." Her eyelids fluttered and her voice dropped to a conspiratorial whisper.

"And he told her he was leaving her. That he wanted a divorce."

"A divorce?" gasped Floria.

"Sh . . . let her finish," said Daisy, sensing Violeta had more to say. She didn't want to interrupt the housekeeper's train of thought.

"Serena screamed at him. I never heard anything like it. It was like she went crazy." She shook her head at the memory. "She demanded to know who he was sleeping with. He told her it was air hostess, someone he meet on a trip to France. He said they were going to the Bahamas, to the house there, and that it is over between them."

Violeta wrung her hands. "I've never seen madam so upset. She sat on landing and cried for hours. I was so worried about her."

Floria took a deep breath. "So, Collin finally worked up the courage to leave her? I didn't think he had the balls. She always ran roughshod over him and he never complained. I suspected it was because he didn't want to rock the boat—well, more so than it was rocking already. But obviously, he'd had enough."

"Everyone has their limits," mused Daisy. "Although I can't say I'm surprised. She practically threw herself at that Russian composer, Vladimir Someone, at the garden party last month. She was all over him on the dance floor. It was positively debauched, and the guy must have been half her age. Don't you remember? Collin had a fit. I thought then that it was the last straw."

"Vladimir Kustov." Floria knew most of her mother's musician friends. "I suppose it was inevitable. Mother's behavior has been out of control this last year, what with the drinking and the tantrums and the sordid affairs. I don't know how Collin put up with it for so long, to be honest. He deserved a medal."

"She was out of her mind with grief," Violeta added. "I don't think she believe he'd leave her. I took her up some tea, but she threw it against the wall and screamed at me to get out. We were going to my daughter's for supper, so I left her alone. If only I'd stayed . . . " She hung her head, the guilt evident on her wrinkled face.

Daisy squeezed Violeta's hand. "It's not your fault. You weren't to know she'd fall over the balustrade."

At that moment, DI McGuinness flung open the kitchen door, which ricocheted off the wall with a resounding bang, giving them all a fright. He'd obviously never heard of knocking either.

"Sorry to interrupt." He took a giant step into the room and glanced around the table. "Do you mind if I ask you some questions?" Daisy noticed the faintest hint of an Irish lilt to his otherwise gravelly voice.

"Go ahead, Inspector. Would you like some tea?" She gestured to a vacant seat opposite her.

"No, thank you." He pulled out the chair and sat down. His long legs collided with hers under the table, but he didn't appear to notice, so she discreetly shifted hers to one side. All eyes were on him as they waited for him to speak.

He hesitated, as if suddenly unsure how to proceed.

It's bad, thought Daisy, sensing this was out of character for the tough detective. He didn't strike her as the emotional type.

He cleared his throat, then his direct gaze settled on Floria. "I'm sorry to have to tell you this, Miss Levanté, but it appears your mother was murdered."

"What?" barked Floria, knocking over her teacup which, thankfully, was almost empty. Remnants of tea spilled out onto the saucer and table, but no one made a move to stop it.

"*Dio mio!*" Violeta crossed herself.

"How do you know she was murdered?" Daisy leaned forward over her cup. The forensic team must have found something.

DI McGuinness met her gaze. "There is evidence of blunt force trauma to the head."

"You mean someone hit her?" Daisy felt the need to clarify.

"That appears to be the case. It'll be confirmed during the postmortem, of course, but that's what it looks like."

"Who would want to kill Mother?" Floria whispered, uncomprehending. The color that had been seeping back into her face had vanished and she clutched the tabletop like she was afraid if she let go she'd topple off her chair.

Collin for one, thought Daisy, although she didn't say as much.

"Is that why she fell?" asked Floria.

"Or was she pushed?" Daisy couldn't help herself. She'd always had a flair for the dramatic. Put it down to too many detective novels.

The inspector glared at her and muttered, "We don't know that for sure yet. Forensics is still working on it."

Yes! Daisy thought triumphantly. Serena had been pushed over the balustrade. The detective's expression said it all.

"I don't believe this." Floria let go of the table and dropped her head into her hands. "I feel like I'm living in a nightmare."

Daisy rubbed her back.

DI McGuinness cleared his throat. It didn't help to allay the gravelliness. I'm afraid I have to ask you all where you were last night."

"Are we suspects now?" Floria's eyes were as wide as the hand-painted saucers under the teacups.

Daisy smiled reassuringly. "It's just procedure, honey. The inspector wants to rule us out."

"Oh."

At his questioning look, she added, "My grandfather was a detective, a Detective Chief Inspector, actually. I spent a lot of time with him growing up." Her folks wouldn't win any parenting awards either.

"I'll start," mumbled Floria. "Last night, I was at a restaurant with my boyfriend, James—or rather ex-boyfriend now. He dumped me. Prick."

DI McGuinness looked startled.

Daisy jumped up. "Oh, sweetie. Why didn't you say?"

"I was going to call you this morning, then all of this happened . . . ." Her voice petered out.

Daisy put her hands on her shoulders, "I'm so sorry. What happened?"

"He called me a bimbo." She sniffed. "Said I was a PR disaster. It was the picture of me in the Jacuzzi that did it. Someone leaked a copy to *The Star*. His bosses told him to get rid of me or he'd lose his job."

"Bastard," huffed Daisy. "He should have defended you, not given in to them. He's a gutless coward." She paused. "Besides, that was a great party."

Floria turned her tearstained face up toward her. "I know, right? And there were loads of us in the Jacuzzi. It wasn't just me."

Daisy was furious. "He's an idiot. You're better off without him."

Violeta nodded in silent agreement. Daisy knew the housekeeper had never approved of Floria's posh, politicking boyfriend either.

DI McGuinness was at a loss for words. The expression on his face was quite comical, and Daisy would have laughed if it wasn't for the seriousness of the situation. He clearly hadn't anticipated the turn in conversation.

"Erm, could you give me the name of the restaurant?"

"Posticino's in South Kensington."

He wrote it down.

"It's very good if you like Italian food," Daisy pointed out. "I recommend the veal limone."

Floria sniffed. "It *is* excellent."

McGuinness didn't reply. The menu was of no consequence to him. Instead, he turned to the housekeeper. "Where were you, Mrs. Bonello?"

"Who, me?" She looked shocked to be asked. The help was usually invisible, at least in Serena's household. "I was at my daughter's house. We—that's my husband and I—go every Saturday after work. We babysit so they can go out. Sunday's our day off, you see."

"But you didn't stay over last night?"

"No, her little one come down with fever, so my daughter thought it best if we didn't stay. Besides, as I tell the girls, I'd forgotten my statins here. That's why I popped in this morning, to get them." She nodded toward the cupboard above the kettle.

"Pepe is the groundskeeper here," explained Floria. "They've both been with us for over twenty years. I've known Violeta since I was ten. There is no way they are involved in this."

"Thank you, Miss Levanté." He turned back to the housekeeper. "Could you give me your daughter's name and address?"

The Italian woman obliged.

Daisy waited her turn. Finally, the inspector turned his attention to her. They might not officially be suspects, but he was gazing at her as if she was one. Up close, she noticed his eyes were an unusual shade of dark gray, like storm clouds moments before the rain poured down. "Now you, Miss Thorne. Where were you last night?"

She pulled her thoughts back to the evening before. "I had to do a group of ladies who were going to see Tom Jones at the racecourse, so I worked late. Once they'd left, I cleaned the salon and got home about eight. I made supper, then watched *Midsomer Murders* until ten. You know, you remind me a bit of Inspector Barnaby, just a much younger version. You have that same intense look about you."

DI McGuinness said wearily, "Can anyone vouch for you?"

"Actually, yes. Mr. Tiddles escaped, so I helped Moira find him. That must have been at about ten thirty. I was getting ready for bed."

"Mr. Tiddles?"

"Moira's cat." At his exasperated expression, she added, "Moira's my neighbor."

"I think I surmised that much, thank you. I'll have to get her address too, if you don't mind."

"No problem." She gave it to him, then added, "I'm the

cottage on the left, number four, if you have any more questions."

"I think that'll do, thank you."

"Daisy's a wealth of information," Floria told him with a little nod to back up her statement. "She knows absolutely everyone."

Daisy smiled. "It's true. I own the hair salon in the High Street. It's the only one in the village. Everyone has been in at some point or another. So, if you want the lowdown on anyone, come and find me. It's called Ooh La La."

DI McGuinness gave her a thoughtful look. "I'll keep that in mind."

Chapter Three

The day after they'd found Dame Serena Levanté's body dawned bright and sunny, as if the universe was trying to forget the dastardly deeds of the day before. Daisy inhaled the fragrant aroma of Mrs. Chandler's yellow roses as she strolled down the lane toward the village High Street. Gill Chandler won the best garden competition every year, much to Daisy's immense frustration. As one of the first houses visitors saw as they drove into Edgemead, Daisy always tried to keep her garden in top-notch condition and bursting with color. First impressions were so important. Except, somehow, Gill's was always better.

This season was no different.

Daisy had barely finished weeding and planting her petunias and Gill's was already in full bloom. She had to admit, it did look extremely pretty.

Ooh La La, Daisy's hair salon and pride and joy—even more so than her garden—was situated two-thirds of the way down the High Street, sandwiched between the Meadows Gallery and a small clothing boutique. She'd bought it after graduating from beauty school with the money her parents had given her before they'd emigrated to Spain. Doing it up had been loads of fun. She'd opted for a shabby chic interior with a large chandelier and real wooden floors. Each station had its own gilt-framed mirror and spot lighting, and she served complimentary cups of tea and coffee and, if she'd had time to bake, perhaps a slice of lemon drizzle cake too.

The basins were situated at the back of the salon, against a wall festooned with elaborate vintage wallpaper, and she'd made certain the reclining chairs for her customers were of the utmost comfort. Being tall, with a long, slender neck, she knew how agonizing leaning back onto a hard basin could be. The result was spectacular, and she was consistently booked up for weeks in advance, although she always managed to squeeze in one or two impromptu appointments during the day.

Krish was already there when she arrived. Apart from her, he was the only other person who had a key to the salon, and she trusted him implicitly. Krish was Indian and gay, a difficult combination in his culture. Like her, his parents had abandoned him, so he'd put himself through hairdressing school and was now one of the most talented stylists she'd ever met. He was also a terrible gossip.

"You have to tell me all about Dame Serena's murder," he said the moment she walked through the door.

"Give me a minute to sort myself out." She laughed, hanging up her bag on the hatstand. "I haven't even had a coffee yet."

"It's all over the village," he persisted. "Is it true she was bashed on the head?"

"I'm afraid so." She swept into the little kitchenette

behind the salon to put the kettle on. Krish followed her like a puppy. If he had a tail, it would be wagging in anticipation. "Do they know whodunit?"

"Not yet, although the detective in charge seems very capable. DI McGuinness, his name is."

"My sources say he's a bit of a dish. Gruff and manly."

Daisy couldn't help but smile. "I'd have to agree with that."

Krish clapped his hands in excitement. "Our very own murder, and a celebrity at that. Of course, it's horrible for Dame Serena, but quite thrilling for the rest of us."

Daisy took her coffee into the salon and sat down on the vintage sofa that her clients used while they were waiting for their appointments. It looked like a 1920s classic, with its turned legs and elegant design, but she'd bought it brand-new from an interior design wholesaler in Cobham shortly after she'd opened. It was the most expensive item in the store, other than the actual equipment, and was one of her favorite pieces. In front of it was a matching footstool that functioned as a magazine rack and newspaper stand. Krish had bought the daily newspapers, like he always did in the morning, and they lay on top of the footstool, crisp and unopened, waiting to be read.

"We shouldn't get too excited," Daisy cautioned as she gazed at Dame Serena's perfectly made-up face staring up at her from the front page of the *Daily Mail*. The photograph must have been taken some time ago. Dame Serena hadn't looked that good in ages. "The murderer is still out there. It could be anyone."

Krish stopped preparing the workstations and gasped, "Do you think we know them? Could they be one of us?"

Krish considered himself a local, and he practically

was now. He lived in a small flat above the newsagent's—the same one he'd moved into three years ago—and apart from weekend jaunts to London, he was always at the salon. He worked hard, he was a genius in the hair department, and her clients loved him, not least because he had the lowdown on everything from Prince William and Kate's latest appearance to which celebrities were hooking up on Love Island.

She shrugged. "I don't know. It's possible, I suppose, but that is for the police to figure out."

Asa was next to arrive. The chatty, Afro-Caribbean girl was only eighteen, and Daisy was training her up to be a junior stylist. At the moment, however, she washed customers' hair and gave them a luxurious head massage before their treatment.

"I heard about Dame Serena. They say the husband done it." She plunked down her bag next to Daisy on the floor. Today, her long nails were a sparkly forest green. How she didn't scalp people with those talons, Daisy had no idea.

"As far as I know, they haven't managed to contact Collin yet." Floria had been asleep when Daisy had left the house this morning, but she had no doubt her friend would pop into the salon to give her an update, if and when she heard anything.

"Can't say I blame him. She was a handful. Cheating on him and everything. I heard he caught her at it with that hot Russian musician. Chased him out of the house in his undies. Can you imagine that?" She burst out laughing.

Daisy gave her a stern look. She'd heard that rumor too, and while scandal surrounding Serena did normally have an essence of truth, it was still just a story. "We don't know who did it yet, and please take your bag into the back. We can't have the customers tripping over it."

Asa grinned and picked up her bag as Penny, the last of her employees to arrive, sauntered in. "Guess what? I've just run into Tatiana, Dame Serena's maid, and she says the police questioned her all evening about a missing painting. Poor thing's beside herself."

"A missing painting?" Daisy stood up. This was a new development, one that the police hadn't divulged yesterday. Floria certainly hadn't mentioned anything about a missing painting. "Are you sure?"

"Yes, she was in pieces. They basically accused her of stealing it. It was quite valuable, apparently. A Mod . . . Mod . . . " She shrugged, unable to remember the artist's name.

"Not the Modigliani?" Daisy was shocked. That piece had been Serena's favorite, a gift from Collin on their wedding day. Not many people knew of its existence for security reasons. "Quite valuable" was a gross understatement. Apart from its sentimental value, the piece was worth tens of millions of pounds. She remembered Floria saying Collin had acquired it in Tuscany, from an old contessa whose family had owned it for generations.

Penny clicked her fingers. "That's it."

"Good heavens! Where's Tatiana now?"

"She's gone into Boots. I think she's looking for eye drops. Her lids are all swollen, poor dear."

Penny looked fantastic, as usual. Her flaming red hair was up in a messy bun, tendrils framing her face. She wore the tiniest shorts, which made her smooth, tanned legs appear endless, with a flouncy, bohemian blouse. An out-of-work model, Penny had turned to hairdressing as a way to supplement her income, but the job had become her staple now and she rarely took on new modeling work. "It's too cutthroat for me," she'd told Daisy during her interview. "I don't have the stomach for it."

"I'll be right back." Daisy dashed out of the store and across the road to Boots. If she could catch Tatiana, she might be able to get a bit more information on the Modigliani. The Russian maid had paid for her items and was wandering down the perfume aisle, a forlorn expression on her face, when Daisy found her.

"Hello, Tatiana. Do you remember me? I'm Floria's friend."

Tatiana glanced up, and Daisy saw at once she was in a state. Her eyes were red-rimmed and bloodshot, her cheeks mottled and her usually glossy hair hung listlessly down her back.

"Oh, yes. Hello." She sniffed. Daisy took her by the arm and steered her across the road.

"I know what you need: a nice cup of tea and a wash and blow-dry. That will make you feel like a new person."

Tatiana tried to resist. "No, I can't afford it. I don't know if you heard, but I'm out of work." Her eyes filled with tears.

"It's on the house," Daisy insisted as she opened the door to the salon. "We open in twenty minutes, so I'll make you a cuppa while Asa works her magic on your hair."

She didn't give the Russian maid time to object. Asa nodded and got to work, while Daisy made the tea. After a relaxing head massage, Daisy led her to a leather-clad chair. "I'll dry it for you. Here's your tea."

"Thank you, you're so nice." Tatiana looked better already. Her cheeks weren't so blotchy, and the deer-in-the-headlights look had gone from her eyes.

"Don't mention it. We girls have to stick together." She began to dry Tatiana's hair using soft, rhythmic motions, and when Tatiana had relaxed into the chair, she asked, "Was it the Modigliani that was stolen from Brompton Court?"

The fearful look came back. "I didn't take it."

"Oh, I know you didn't," Daisy was quick to reassure her. "Don't worry about that. I'm just shocked it was stolen, that's all. It was worth so much money."

"How much?" Tatiana asked, meeting her gaze in the mirror.

"Oh, millions," Daisy replied. "I know one of Modigliani's reclining nudes sold for over a hundred and fifty million pounds at auction last year. Serena's wasn't as well-known as that one, but you get the picture."

Tatiana gasped, her eyes out on stalks. "Really? That much? No wonder the police were so concerned. They said it was why Dame Serena was murdered."

"A burglary gone wrong?"

"I think so."

That put a different spin on things. Collin wouldn't have stolen his own painting, even though he'd given it to Serena, unless he was afraid he wouldn't get it back if they divorced. She thought about that for a moment. It was a distinct possibility, but why now? Why after this fight, when they weren't even divorced yet? From her understanding, Collin had only announced his intention to divorce Serena the day before her death. No, it was more likely a robber who Serena had caught in the act. How gruesome. A shiver ran unbidden down her spine, and she was grateful for the warmth of the hair dryer in her hand. "Was it DI McGuinness who interviewed you last night?"

Tatiana's shoulders tensed up. "Yes, and he wasn't very nice either. He kept asking the same questions over and over again, like where was I the night of the murder? And could anyone vouch for me?"

"He asked me that too," Daisy told her, rolling her long hair around the brush and holding it in front of the dryer.

Tatiana's eyes widened. "Really? You were also questioned?"

"Yes. I arrived shortly after Dame Serena's body was found. They're questioning everyone who knew Serena; it's just procedure."

Tatiana looked down at her hands. "I don't trust the police. In Russia, they are the bad guys."

"Our police aren't like that. Here, they're the good guys."

The look on Tatiana's face said she didn't believe that for an instant.

"So, did you tell them?" Daisy rolled more hair around the dryer.

"Tell them what?"

"Where you were the night of the murder? You don't live on the premises, do you?"

She scoffed. "Of course not. Serena would never let me, even though there is plenty of room in that old house. I live in Surbiton with my boyfriend, Sergio. I catch the train to work every day."

"Ah, I see. So, Sergio can vouch for you, then?" She

was fishing, hoping Tatiana trusted her enough to take the bait.

"Yes, of course. We were home together. He made dinner and I painted my nails. Look."

She held out her hands for Daisy to inspect.

"That's actually a very good job," Daisy remarked, admiring the short, neat nails painted in pastel blue. Asa poked her head over Daisy's shoulder to take a peek too. Nails were her thing. In fact, Daisy had been toying with the idea of adding a nail bar to the salon and letting Asa manage it.

"What did you have for dinner?"

"Huh?"

"You said Sergio cooked. I'm very impressed. My last boyfriend couldn't cook to save his life." She gave a sheepish grin.

Tatiana shrugged. "Sergio's father is a chef in Poland. We had sirloin steak. Anyway, I told the detective we were home, but I don't think he believed me."

Daisy met her gaze in the mirror. "It doesn't matter what he believes. If you didn't do it, you don't need to worry."

Tatiana looked away.

"I know."

Chapter Four

At midday, Floria snuck into the salon to see Daisy. Immediately, she was swamped by well-wishers and those who were assuaging their curiosity and couldn't believe their luck that the subject of the latest village gossip was now standing in front of them.

"So sorry to hear about your mother, Floria," said Beatrice, the baker's wife, who was waiting for her hair appointment. "Such a horrible way to go."

"Thank you," murmured Floria, looking around for Daisy. The salon was busier than usual, with a queue of walk-ins and regulars fighting for last-minute appointments. The phone rang unanswered. Both Penny and Krish were elbow-deep in tint and Asa was furiously washing hair, sending suds flying out of the ceramic sink.

"She'll be sorely missed," yelled Mrs. Bryson from under the hair dryer.

"Such a talent," said kindly Mrs. Robbins, who spent the majority of her state pension on tickets to the Royal Opera. "What a marvelous voice."

Daisy emerged from the tiny kitchen at the back of the shop carrying a bowl filled with sharp-smelling gray gunge. "Hi darling, give me a sec. I'm just about to do Yvette's highlights."

Yvette, the stylish Frenchwoman who owned the clothing boutique next door, beckoned to Floria from her position in front of the mirror. "Come and talk to us, Floria," she said. "I'm dying to know what happened to your mother. Was it really murder?"

"That's what they're saying," said Floria vaguely, casting a desperate look at Daisy.

"It's an ongoing investigation, Yvette," Daisy reminded her. "We can't talk about it."

"Of course." Yvette met Daisy's gaze in the mirror. She looked proud of herself, like she knew something no one else did and was waiting to see the reaction. "I bumped into Tatiana on my way in and she told me about the missing painting."

Daisy could tell by Floria's expression that this wasn't a surprise. Yvette looked disappointed.

"You know about the Modigliani?" Daisy asked her friend.

Floria nodded. "DI McGuinness called me this morning and told me about the burglary. I don't know what to make of it. Collin will be gutted."

"Well, I would have thought it was obvious, *mon ami*," said Yvette. "A thief broke into the house to steal the objet d'art and killed your mother in the process." She shook her head, making the foil wraps rustle. "It's never a good idea to have such valuable art on display. They really should have known better. I keep all my valuables locked away in my safe." She touched the strand of pearls hanging around her neck.

"Keep still," instructed Daisy, pausing with the brush in the air.

"Did you say a thief?" shouted Mrs. Bryson from under the dryer.

"Five more minutes, Mrs. B." Krish dashed over and embraced Floria. "Darling, I'm so sorry. I know she was a complete bitch, but it's never easy, is it?" He kissed Floria on both cheeks.

"Thank you," mumbled Floria.

"Krish, can you take over for a sec? I want to make Floria a cup of tea in the back. She looks like she needs one."

"I'm okay," insisted Floria. "I just popped in to say hi. I can see you guys are busy."

"Nonsense, go and have a brew," ordered Krish, taking the brush from Daisy. "Yvette doesn't mind, do you, love?"

Daisy didn't hear Yvette's reply as she shepherded Floria into the tiny kitchenette. As soon as they were out of sight, she turned to her friend. "I'm sorry about all that. Everybody wants to find out what happened. This is the most exciting thing that's happened in Edgemead for decades." She frowned as she took in Floria's grim expression. "But tell me, how are you holding up?"

The two of them had stayed up late last night, drinking wine and talking about Serena. Floria's relationship with her mother had been tumultuous at best and she'd needed to vent. The emotions of the day had unlocked far more than grief.

"I can't help feeling I should be more upset she's dead," Floria had said at one point during the evening. "Do you think there's something wrong with me?"

"Of course not," Daisy was quick to reassure her. "Let's

face it, Serena wasn't a mother to you. She was a celebrity who flitted in and out of your life. When you were a baby, she abandoned you to nannies and housekeepers, and when you were old enough, she shipped you off to boarding school. You never had a relationship with her, so it's hard to feel anything now that she's gone."

Floria thought about that for a moment. "You know, if you ever want a change in career, you'd make a great shrink."

"Why do you think I'm studying forensic psychology?" Daisy's eyes gleamed. "I love analyzing people."

"You wouldn't leave the salon, would you?" asked Floria worriedly. "I know how much this place means to you."

"God, no, but I might take on some extra work, like helping the police profile suspects, that sort of thing. I've always found it fascinating."

Floria tilted her head to the side. "I can see you doing that, and you're right about what you said about Mother and me. All she was ever interested in was her singing career. I don't think she loved me at all." Her friend's lip quivered, but she kept it together. Daisy knew how hard it was for her to accept that. "I can't remember her coming to one sports day or school performance. Not one. What kind of mother doesn't do that?"

"It's unforgivable," Daisy acknowledged. Floria didn't mind her being so direct. They'd spoken about Serena many times before, and in Daisy's opinion, the neglect and plain disinterest she'd shown her daughter over the years was abominable. "If it helps, I don't think she even knew who I was."

Floria laughed, rather too easily. "No, she was even less

interested in my friends." She took another gulp of the bordeaux and looked Daisy in the eye. "You know what? I'm not sorry she's dead. She was a horrible woman and a terrible mother. I won't mourn her."

It was the wine talking. Deep down, Daisy knew her friend was devastated. Serena had been a true star. Her phenomenal voice had brought joy to millions of people, and her albums still topped the classical music charts. Her vivacious and tempestuous personality had enthralled and shocked the press and public alike, and her strikingly beautiful face had adorned the pages of all the glossy magazines at one time or another. Her loss would be felt all over the music industry, if not by her own family.

Daisy put on the kettle and got down two cups and saucers from the shelf. "So, did the inspector say anything else?"

Floria shook her head. "No, but he wants to meet me at the Scout hall at three o'clock. Apparently, he has some news."

"That sounds promising, but why the Scout hall?"

"That's where they've set up shop."

"I see." She supposed they had to have an incident room somewhere. Edgemead didn't even have its own police station—they used the one in Esher—but the nearest criminal investigation department was probably Guildford, about fourteen miles and a good half hour's drive away. She put two tea bags into the cups and filled them up with boiling water. Then she got the milk out of the fridge.

Floria grabbed her arm. "Will you come with me, Dais? I don't think I can face him alone. He's so intimidating. Just the way he looks at me makes me feel guilty, and I've done nothing wrong."

Daisy chortled. "He's not so bad."

"Please?"

"I'll try. We've been pretty manic today; more so than usual. I think everyone has come here to find out what happened."

Floria shook her head. "Murder is good for business."

"That it is." Daisy finished making the tea and handed her friend a cup. "Get that down you. It'll make you feel better."

Floria gripped the handle without taking a sip. "I wonder what news DI McGuinness has? Nothing bad, I hope. I don't think I could stomach any more bad news."

"If it's a development, it can only be good news." Daisy forced a smile. "It means they are that much closer to catching who did this."

"I hope so," muttered Floria, finally taking a sip. She shut her eyes momentarily, savoring the sweetness. "God, I needed this."

"I was thinking," said Daisy. "There are only a handful of people who knew Serena was alone that night. Tatiana, Violeta and Pepe and Collin."

Floria perked up. "DI McGuinness said there was no sign of a break-in, so either the murderer had a key or Mother let him in of her own free will."

Daisy leaned back against the countertop. "So, either way, she knew her attacker."

"Do you think it was one of them?" whispered Floria. The hand holding the teacup trembled ever so slightly.

"I know the police are looking at Tatiana and her boyfriend—Sergio, I think his name is. I had her in here earlier, frightened out of her wits. Apparently, they'd been questioned all night."

"Really? But why would they want to hurt Mother?"

Daisy pursed her lips. "It may not have been intentional. Perhaps she interrupted them?"

Floria frowned. "It's possible, I suppose. One thing I know for sure is that Violeta and Pepe wouldn't be capable of something like this."

Daisy nodded.

Floria continued pensively, "Which leaves Collin."

"Except he was away, according to Violeta."

Floria sighed. "Okay, so maybe they are on the right track with Tatiana and her boyfriend."

They stared at each other for a long moment, then Floria gasped. "Oh, Lord. I remember something else."

"What?"

"Something Greg said."

"Greg? Your friend, Greg?"

"Yes, he's Mother's solicitor and the executor of her estate. He also called me this morning. Apparently, Mother had made an appointment to change her will."

Daisy slowly put down her cup. "Floria, that is an important piece of information. Don't you see? She calls Greg to change her will and the day before her appointment, she's murdered."

Floria grabbed the fridge for support. "It's related, isn't it?"

Daisy felt a surge of adrenaline. "Maybe. I don't know yet, but it's a hell of a coincidence, don't you think? Did Greg say why she wanted to change it?"

Floria grimaced. "No, he didn't, and I don't even know what's in her current will. He hasn't shown me a copy yet.

Apparently, there are a few things he has to take care of first. It's all very mysterious."

Daisy frowned. "Hmm . . . I wonder who stands to inherit? You, obviously, but what about Collin?" She gasped as a thought occurred to her.

"What?" Floria nearly spilled her tea.

"I wonder if Serena was going to cut Collin out of her will? We know they were having marital problems. She'd been unfaithful before and he had a lover, the air hostess. Things were hardly ideal between them."

"Far from it. They fought like cats and dogs," muttered Floria.

Daisy's forehead furrowed. "How is this for a theory? Collin wanted to divorce her, but he knew he wouldn't inherit anything if he did. Stealing the painting could have been a ruse, a ploy to distract attention away from himself."

"Do you think so?" Floria's voice trembled. "If she divorced him, he wouldn't get a penny. They signed a prenup. Greg told me at their wedding."

"Exactly! So, he killed her first."

Floria stared at her. "We've got to tell DI McGuinness."

The Scout hall was situated on the outskirts of the village. It took the form of a modern, wooden barn with a garage-style, roll-up door painted olive green. It backed onto a large meadow, with sleepy cows grazing in it. Beyond that, the Thames flowed idly by, curving through the landscape like a thick, silver ribbon. It was an ideal location for little boys and girls to explore the outdoors. As a teenager, Daisy had joined the Girl Guides and spent many a happy summer making friends and participating in activities outdoors and on the river. She'd learned canoeing and sailing, how to administer first aid, and how to read a map, plus it got her out of the house and away from her golf-obsessed parents who, quite frankly, wouldn't have cared what she'd done as long as it got her out from under their noses.

The garage door was half open, so they bent down and slipped underneath. The familiar smell of pine and chalk transported her back to those hazy summer days, and she took a moment to soak it all in: the vibrant maps and nature posters on the walls, the well-worn floorboards and the beams in the rafters that had seemed so high when she was young but were actually quite average.

DI McGuinness was in earnest conversation with a tall, handsome man with ash-blond hair at the front of the hall and hadn't noticed them yet.

"Hello, Inspector," Daisy called out. "Do you mind if we come in?"

He spun around. "Miss Thorne, you shouldn't be here. This is our incident room. It's off-limits to the public."

"Greg? What are you doing here?" Floria walked forward and gave her old friend a hug. His response was lackluster. "What's wrong?"

"I was just talking to DI McGuinness about the matter of your mother's will," he said, clearly uncomfortable. He couldn't meet her gaze.

Daisy joined them, ignoring the pained look from McGuinness. There was a large photograph of Serena pinned to a whiteboard at the front of the hall, along with a smaller one of her dead body as it had been found at the foot of the stairs. It was the first time Daisy had seen the crime scene, and she found she couldn't drag her eyes away from it.

Serena was fully dressed in a tight skirt and a blouse stained with what could be blood or red wine, but probably the former. Violeta had said it was a whiskey bottle that had been found on the landing. When Serena was on a binge, that was her drink of choice. The unnatural angle of her neck was the telltale sign. Her vacant eyes stared up at the ceiling, or perhaps at the landing where her assailant had stood. The look on her face was one of abject horror.

Daisy shuddered. Floria hadn't seen it yet; she was too preoccupied with Greg's strange behavior. Beside the photographs, the detective had written down their suspects. Daisy perused the list. Along with the obvious ones Daisy and Floria had discussed, he'd added all three of Serena's ex-husbands.

Hmm . . . Why them? As far as Daisy knew, there was no bad blood between Serena and any of her exes, but then, McGuinness didn't know that. He was probably covering the bases.

"We heard she wanted to change it." Daisy's eyes were still on the board.

DI McGuinness angled himself so he blocked her line of sight.

Greg replied, "Yes, that's true, but she didn't, so the current will and testament still stands."

"Is there something wrong with it?" Floria asked. When he didn't respond, she tugged his arm. "Greg, this is me. Please tell me what's going on."

Greg glanced at DI McGuinness, who sighed and gave a small nod.

"There's something I have to tell you, Floria, and I fear it's going to come as a shock."

"Oh, for goodness' sake. What is it?" Daisy was losing patience. The anticipation was killing her.

"Okay, here goes." He turned Floria to face him, placing his hands on her shoulders. "You weren't Serena's only child, Flo. She had three illegitimate daughters before you were born."

"What?" cried Floria and Daisy simultaneously.

Greg took a step back and put up his hands. "I'm sorry. I wanted to tell you so many times, but I was sworn to secrecy by Serena. It was part of our client confidentiality agreement. I would have been sacked if I'd said anything."

Floria was at a loss for words. She was mouthing like a guppy. Daisy couldn't blame her. She'd just discovered she had three half sisters. It was unbelievable. Even Daisy found it hard to grasp, but she found her tongue first. "Where are these women now?"

"That's what I've been trying to do since Serena's death, but tracking them down hasn't been easy. One lives in Australia, the other Spain and the third Austria. They're scattered all over the globe."

"I have three sisters?" Floria looked like she might faint.

An only child herself, Daisy could imagine the myriad of emotions her friend must be feeling. She maneuvered her to the nearest chair. "Here, sit down for a moment." Floria flopped into it like a rag doll.

She shook her head from side to side, making her blond curls bounce. "I don't believe it. How could Mother have kept this a secret all these years?"

"Half sisters," corrected Greg, a stickler for detail. "I

have now managed to contact all three of them and they're flying to London in the next few days. It was your mother's wish that they all attend her funeral, followed by the reading of the will."

"Memorial service," corrected McGuinness. "We haven't released the body yet."

"Do they all stand to inherit?" asked Daisy, thinking her suspect list was growing by the minute.

"I'm afraid I can't say," Greg replied.

The inspector's eyes seemed overly bright. Daisy tilted her head to the side. "But you know, don't you, Inspector?"

He gave her a hard glare. "Of course I know, but I had to get a warrant."

What she would do to find out! They had to assume all three illegitimate sisters were going to inherit part of Serena's vast fortune, otherwise why had Serena requested their presence? Although Floria wasn't thinking about that. "I can't believe I've got three sisters," she whispered, staring into the middle distance like she was in a trance.

Daisy hugged her, bringing her back to reality. "I'm so happy for you, Floria. This is wonderful news." She turned to Greg. "Do they know Serena is—sorry, was—their mother?"

He scratched his chin. "Two definitely didn't know. I think it shocked the hell out of them. The third, the Spanish one, she might have known. She didn't sound all that surprised, although she wasn't interested in coming to the memorial service. I had to tell her it was nonnegotiable."

"Another three suspects for your list, Inspector." Daisy nodded toward the whiteboard. DI McGuinness didn't reply.

"What are their names?" Floria's voice trembled. Daisy

could see she was desperate for information, and who wouldn't be? For thirty years she'd grown up believing she was an only child, only to discover she had three half sisters who, right now, were preparing to come to London.

"Why don't you and Greg go for a drink?" Daisy suggested. Then to Greg, "I'm sure Floria could use one after that bombshell."

Greg nodded, eager to make up for withholding the information from Floria. "Great idea. My car's out front."

"You can tell me all about it later." Daisy gave Floria's hand a squeeze. "I've got to get back to the salon."

Once they'd left, Daisy turned to DI McGuinness. "Well, that *was* a bombshell."

He didn't react. "Is there something else I can help you with, Miss Thorne?"

He was a hard nut to crack. Personally, she didn't think it would hurt to be a bit friendlier. She flashed him her brightest smile and said, "I know you're busy, but we have a theory you might like to hear."

DI McGuinness sank his lanky form into the chair previously occupied by Floria. There were shadows under his eyes, and he had the beginnings of a five-o'clock shadow. She was willing to bet he'd pulled an all-nighter. She knew from watching reality TV how important the first twenty-four hours in a murder investigation were.

"Go ahead, Miss Thorne. I'm all ears."

"Please, call me Daisy. 'Miss Thorne' makes me sound like a schoolteacher."

He acknowledged her request with a little tilt of his head.

She perched on the edge of a desk, her long legs stretched out in front of her. "So, Greg mentioned to

Floria that Serena wanted to change her will. Now granted, we didn't know about her three illegitimate daughters at the time, but we were wondering if she might have wanted to cut Collin out of her will. They were having marital problems, you see. Both had had or were having affairs. Perhaps she was planning to divorce him?"

McGuinness studied her, his eyes narrowed. "And you think he found out about it, which gave him a motive for killing her?"

Some of the wind went out of Daisy's sails. "You've already thought of that, haven't you?"

He gave a small grin, the first she'd seen. It made his face far less severe, and she liked the way his eyes crinkled at the edges.

She asked, "Did Greg say what Serena wanted to change?"

The inspector stood up. "Unfortunately, no. She didn't specify. But she could have intended to cut her three illegitimate daughters out of the will, which would give them a motive too."

Daisy got to her feet too. "Except none of them were in London at the time of the murder."

His expression turned thoughtful. "None that we know of, but Spain and Austria are only a short flight away. I always expect the unexpected. Granted, Australia is more of a stretch. We can probably discount that one."

Daisy was inclined to agree. "Have you located Collin yet?"

"No, we're still looking. His phone is off, so we can't ping it, unfortunately, but as soon as he turns it back on, we'll get a fix on him."

Daisy was impressed. "Well, I'm sorry we bothered you. It seems you're following up on all the angles."

He allowed himself another small smile as he escorted her to the door. "Thanks for coming by. If I need you, I know where to find you." In other words: don't come around again.

She smiled. "Okay, Detective Inspector. I get the message. But just so you know, I'm not going to stop asking questions. Floria is one of my best friends and anything I can do to help find out who did this, I will."

McGuinness's eyes lost their crinkles. "Don't get in the way, Miss Thorne. This isn't my first murder case. I know what I'm doing. I understand you want to help, but snooping around isn't going to do that. You could be putting yourself and your friend in danger. If you hear of anything important, by all means, let me know. Otherwise, please stay out of it."

Daisy left the Scout hall feeling suitably chastised. DI McGuinness had warned her off in no uncertain terms; however, she had no intention of listening to him, and if he was half as intelligent as he seemed to be, he'd know she wasn't going to back off either.

Chapter Five

Daisy's two o'clock was a young woman named Sophie who was getting married in a fortnight and wanted to try out wedding hairdos. Daisy loved experimenting with different styles, so she'd blocked out an hour to dedicate to the task. Krish was doing a complicated color job on a middle-aged woman who'd decided she'd had enough of being a bottle blonde and was going back to her natural dark roots and Penny was giving a regular customer a trim.

"Asa, darling, won't you bring us some prosecco?" Daisy smiled at her client. "Wedding preparations always call for bubbles."

Sophie giggled. "Jamie's at a football match, so he won't mind. At least we'll be tidily together when he gets home."

Daisy got to work. She was a good listener and asked all about the wedding arrangements. Sophie was only too happy to talk.

"We're getting married at Polesden Lacey. Have you been there? It's this lovely country house with magnificent gardens and a stunning view for the wedding photos. We've hired the ballroom for the reception, in case it rains.

One can't be too careful in this country." Daisy let her ramble on, asking intermittent questions about her dress, the bridesmaids and, of course, the groom. They were finishing up, having settled on a pretty updo with tendrils dangling on either side of the face, when Sophie said, "I'm so glad we're having the wedding in England. A friend of mine had hers in Italy and the groom got so drunk at the stag party that he missed the flight. It was dreadful. There we all were, waiting at the church, and he didn't arrive. God, what a nightmare."

Daisy stared into space. Sophie's words had sparked an idea.

"Daisy? Are you okay?"

"Oh, sorry. Yes, I'm fine. You just reminded me of something, that's all."

As soon as Sophie had gone, Daisy sat on the couch with her half-empty glass of prosecco and gazed into the effervescence, deep in thought.

"What's up?" Penny asked, having finished with her customer too. Her next appointment was running late.

"What if Collin didn't go to the Bahamas?" Daisy mused.

"Are you talking about Dame Serena's husband?" Penny sat down next to her.

Daisy nodded. "It was something Sophie said. What if he missed his plane? Or didn't go at all? It could have been a ruse to give himself an alibi."

Penny gasped. "You think he's the murderer?"

Daisy pulled herself out of her trance. She didn't want to start spreading rumors. "No, I don't. It was just a thought. I wish there was a way of checking whether he was on that plane or not." She could ask DI McGuinness, but he'd think she was interfering again, and he may have already checked the flights. If he had, he certainly wouldn't share the information with her.

Asa stopped sweeping and said, "I have an auntie who works at Heathrow. I could ask her to check the passenger list."

Daisy jumped up. "Can she do that? I wouldn't want her to get into any trouble."

Asa shrugged. "She works at the BA desk. I'm sure she could look it up on the system. Shall I ask her?"

"Yes, please. Can you call her now?"

"I could, but Mrs. Boxer is here for her perm." She glanced at the door as a smartly dressed woman with a shock of frizzy hair walked in.

"I'll take over. You make the call. It's important, Asa."

Asa came back a few minutes later. "I left a message on her phone. She'll check it during her break and get back to me."

"Great." Daisy finished washing Mrs. Boxer's hair and handed her over to Asa for the massage.

"Guess who I saw with Tatiana at the café this morning?" Krish fanned himself with his hand. "Her Polish boyfriend, Sergio, and oh my goodness, he's hot."

"Really?" Asa was all ears. Even Mrs. Boxer had perked up.

"Yeah, he looks like a gypsy, with long, wild hair and an earring. But that bone structure, phew!"

Daisy couldn't help smiling. "I'd like to have a word with him."

Krish grinned. "I bet you would, you naughty girl. Well, I happen to know where he works, and if you give me Friday afternoon off, I'll tell you."

"That's blackmail." She turned to Penny, who was

setting up the equipment for Mrs. Boxer's perm. "My own staff are blackmailing me."

"It's Dave's birthday party on Saturday night and I want to go shopping in London." Dave was Krish's latest beau. "I've got to get him something decent."

"You can have Thursday afternoon off. Friday is Serena's memorial service and you're all invited to the reception afterward at Brompton Court."

After the whoops had died down she asked, "Now, where does Sergio work?"

"The Buddha Bar in Surbiton." Krish looked smug. "Do you need some company?"

"I don't think so, darling. This won't require a wingman. I just want to ask him some questions about the night Serena was killed."

"Suit yourself. Be sure to tell him I say hi." He winked at Daisy, who rolled her eyes.

A pink-cheeked Floria rushed in, almost tripping over the doormat in her haste. "Oh, Daisy, you won't believe it. All of my sisters are so musical, it's crazy. Mimi's a backup singer, Donna is a violinist and the Spanish one, Carmen, is an opera singer like Mother! I've seen photographs of them; they're all stunning. I can't believe they're going to be here in a few days."

Daisy laughed. "Come and sit down. I'll get you a glass. This is cause for celebration."

"Are you sure you should be celebrating when Dame Serena has just been bumped off?" Krish looked doubtful. "It seems wrong somehow."

"Oh, don't be silly. This is good news. Besides, we've already opened a bottle. It would be a shame to let it go flat. Come and grab a glass. You too, Asa. Pen, I'll leave yours here. We could all do with a little pick-me-up."

Mrs. Boxer got a glass of prosecco too, much to her delight, then Penny got to work on her perm, while the others sat around discussing the new additions to the Levanté family.

"Is it true the Spanish one has a voice like Serena?" asked Asa, who spent too many hours with her nose buried in the tabloids. The pages were awash with minor details of the girls' lives and grainy photographs taken from the internet, but as yet no one had managed to secure an interview with any of them. Greg had advised the girls not to speak to any journalists until after the memorial service, and because they were all traveling to London from abroad, tracking them down would prove rather difficult.

"I couldn't find any clips of her on YouTube, so I don't know." Floria shrugged, then she smiled. "But there were some of Donna, the violinist. Gosh, she's talented. Mesmerizing, actually. She tackled Bartok's solo violin sonata like it was 'Twinkle Twinkle Little Star,' and I've seen professionals struggle with that piece." Thanks to her previous job as an assistant at one of London's biggest classical music production companies, Floria recognized talent when she saw it. "And there's a cringeworthy clip of Mimi's band, Toxic Phonix, but . . . " she paused for effect, "that doesn't mean Mimi isn't any good." That was Floria, loyal to a fault, and she hadn't even met her sisters yet. Daisy only hoped they'd be as welcoming to her.

Asa's phone rang and they all fell silent.

Who's that? mouthed Floria as Asa dashed outside to answer it.

"Her auntie," whispered Krish. "She's checking to see whether Collin made his flight to the Bahamas."

After what seemed like an eternity, Asa came back into the salon, a triumphant look on her face. "You're incredible, you know that, Daisy?"

"He didn't make the flight?"

She shook her head. "Nope. He was never on the flight. Auntie looked up all the passengers flying to Nassau via British Airways on Sunday morning. No Collin Harrison."

"Could he have taken a later flight, or used another airline?"

"He's an Executive Club member," said Floria. "He wouldn't fly another airline."

"There's only one BA flight to Nassau per day," said Asa. "And he wasn't on it."

They all stared at one another, then Daisy spoke. "If Collin didn't go to the Bahamas, then where is he?"

The Buddha Bar in Surbiton was a modern cocktail bar with exposed stonework, a Buddha head at the entrance, lots of greenery and a covered outdoor terrace. A sign at the bar read "Mojito and Martini Mondays." Daisy studied the two bartenders and headed for the best-looking one. Man bun. Earring. Great bone structure. It had to be Sergio.

"Hi, I'm Daisy Thorne," she said, giving him a disarming grin. "I'm a friend of Tatiana's." It was a bit of a stretch, but Sergio wouldn't know.

He smiled tentatively. "What can I get you?"

Up close, she could see what Krish had meant. He was hot, as he'd put it, with those high cheekbones, slanting eyes and full lips, but there was something feral about him, an air of danger. Perhaps it was the suspicious gaze or the earring that gave him a gypsy-like appearance, or maybe it was just the dim light in the bar and her imagination playing tricks on her.

She ordered a mojito and took a seat at the bar. While he prepared it, not without a certain flourish, she pretended to make small talk. "Awful business about Dame Serena, wasn't it? I spoke to Tatiana this morning and she seemed very upset. Apparently, she'd been questioned by the cops."

His eyes narrowed. "They questioned me too."

"And me." Daisy shrugged. "I guess they're just doing their job."

He scoffed. "The police always get it wrong. We told them we were home together on Saturday night."

"Yes, Tatiana said. How was the steak?"

"What?" He looked confused.

"You know, the steak you made for supper?"

"I'm sorry, I have no idea what you're talking about." He placed her drink in front of her.

She shrugged. "Never mind. It was something Tatiana said, but I must have misunderstood."

He was frowning at her, his dark eyes glinting dangerously.

She slid off the barstool and shot him a parting smile. "Thanks again for the drink." She'd made him suspicious. If he mentioned this to Tatiana, they'd realize she'd set him up, which wasn't necessarily a bad thing. If he had something to hide, he ought to be nervous. As her grandfather had often said, sometimes you've got to shake the tree to see what falls down.

DI McGuinness's warning echoed in her ears. *You could be putting yourself and your friend in danger.*

Was Sergio dangerous? Hmm . . . she wasn't sure, but better not stick around to find out. Trying to act normally, she strolled outside onto the small cobblestoned terrace. Tall potted plants flanked the perimeter, giving it a tropical feel ideally suited to the warm weather they'd been having. There weren't many people about, just a couple at the far table enjoying their martinis and a burly security guard standing on the other side of the potted plants, near the exit. She sat down on one of the benches and took a sip of her drink. It wasn't a bad mojito, actually. Glancing inside, she saw Sergio serving another customer. He seemed oblivious to the fact she was still there. Good. Relaxing a little, she pulled out her phone to text Floria.

Sergio wasn't at home on Saturday night. His alibi doesn't check out.

Chapter Six

As she walked to work the next morning, Daisy paused to admire the myriad of daffodils that had sprung up seemingly overnight. They were everywhere, from the central reservation to cottage gardens and in the fields beyond. The stiff breeze made them dance back and forth like ballerinas in bright-yellow tutus.

"Bless you," she said as she passed Mrs. Firth, the librarian, who was rummaging up her sleeve for a tissue. The air fizzed with pollen from the birch and ash trees, made worse by the wind and unexpected high temperatures.

Daisy unlocked the door to Ooh La La and allowed herself a moment of pride. The morning sun shone through the glass front onto the wooden floorboards, turning them a rich mahogany. Shards of light flickered off the vintage chandelier, causing tiny, multicolored flecks to bounce off the walls. To say she was proud of her hair salon was an understatement. When her parents had sent her off to beauty school, saying she'd never amount to much, she'd been determined to prove them wrong. And she had. She now ran a thriving local business and was an established member of the community. Not that her parents were aware. They lived the high life on a golf estate in the Costa del Sol, and Daisy doubted they gave her a second thought.

She sighed.

It was what it was, and it didn't bother her too much. Like Floria, she'd never experienced any particular affection from her parents, and what you never had, you couldn't miss.

Ruth, her eight o'clock, arrived a short time later with wet hair hidden beneath a paisley scarf. The receptionist at the local doctor's office, she popped in before work on Tuesday and Friday to have her hair styled and blow-dried, but she always washed it at home beforehand to save time.

"I've just put the kettle on, Ruth." Daisy motioned for her to take a seat at one of the workstations. "I'll make us some coffee and be with you in a moment."

"Isn't this pollen dreadful?" Ruth sniffed as Daisy handed her a mug. "I've taken two antihistamines and I still can't stop sneezing. Any more and I'll fall asleep at my desk."

Daisy murmured sympathetically. It didn't affect her, but out here in the countryside, surrounded by meadows, it was a real problem for hay fever sufferers.

"How are things at the doctor's office?" Daisy asked. Ruth's occupation, a bit like hers, meant she knew a lot about the private lives of the local community.

"Doris finally retired. We had her farewell last Saturday. It was quite emotional, as she'd been at the office for over thirty years. But it was time; she'd been forgetting things, like passing on messages or getting back to patients."

"Isn't she nearly seventy?"

"Yes, way past retirement age. I think they kept her on out of sympathy, poor thing. So, we're a bit short-staffed until we find a replacement. Luckily, the flu season is over, else we'd never cope."

Daisy applied a leave-in conditioner and combed out the tangles. Ruth had thick, frizzy hair and without her biweekly blow-dry was convinced she'd be walking around with an Afro.

"I heard about Serena's three illegitimate daughters," she said conspiratorially. "She kept that very close to her chest, didn't she?"

News traveled fast in small villages.

Daisy grinned. "Floria is delighted."

"I'm sure she is. As remarkable as Dame Serena was, the woman wasn't fit to be a mother. I don't know why she had one child, let alone four."

"It does boggle the mind." Daisy had wondered the same thing. For a woman so set on a singing career, she'd certainly wasted a lot of time being pregnant and having children.

"She was very beautiful, though," she said wistfully. "I suppose men threw themselves at her. She was probably spoiled for choice."

"Two are twins, I believe." Daisy didn't think Floria would mind her sharing the news. It wouldn't be long before the whole village knew anyway, especially with the girls in question on their way.

"Really?" Ruth was about to ask another question, but a sneeze prevented her from doing so. Daisy switched on the hair dryer. She was finishing up when Ruth said, "Dame Serena's groundskeeper, Mr. Bonello, came to see the doctor yesterday. He's got such bad rheumatism, poor man."

"I wasn't aware." Violeta hadn't mentioned it.

"Oh, yes. His hands are all crumpled up. He can hardly hold his tools anymore. He was concerned he might lose his job, especially now Serena's gone."

"Oh, I'm sure the family won't dismiss him. The Bonellos have worked there for decades. The place wouldn't run without them."

Ruth shrugged. "Still, who knows who will inherit it now? If it's darling Floria, they should be okay, but that Collin is a piece of work. I wouldn't be surprised if he kicks them out before Serena's cold in her grave."

That was a chilling thought. Would Collin really inherit Brompton Court? Floria would be devastated. Not for the first time, Daisy wished she knew what was in the existing will.

Ruth continued. "The doc says Pepe needs an operation, but you know how appalling the waiting times are these days. It's unlikely he'll get something in the next few months. By then, I doubt he'll have much movement left."

"That's terrible. I'll have a chat with Floria to see if she knows anything."

Ruth paid and left, keen to get to the office before it opened at nine.

As she'd cleaned up, Daisy pondered what Ruth had said about Pepe's rheumatism and why Violeta had never mentioned it before. Was it possible they had conspired to steal the Modigliani to pay for private medical care? Had Serena caught them in the act?

It was a crazy notion, and one she was hesitant to run by Floria. It felt like a betrayal. Daisy knew how much

Floria loved Violeta. The maternal housekeeper had been instrumental in her upbringing, particularly in the early years, before Floria had been dispatched to boarding school, and again, during the summer holidays when Floria had no choice but to go home. Violeta had sheltered Floria from her mother's temper tantrums, shielded her from her violent mood swings and provided a shoulder to cry on when Floria had inevitably got in the way. Daisy remembered her friend telling her how she used to stay with Violeta and Pepe at their cottage on the estate when Serena and whichever husband was in residence at the time had a row, or she'd been entertaining a lover and hadn't wanted Floria around.

But now Serena was gone and the Bonellos' livelihood was in jeopardy, would they resort to theft and, inadvertently, murder?

Chapter Seven

As soon as Daisy saw "Unknown Caller" on her phone, she knew it was Detective Inspector McGuinness ringing.

"Good morning, Inspector."

There was a slight pause. "Good guess, Miss Thorne. I wonder if you'd be able to meet me at the Scouts' hall. I want to pick your brain about something."

Now that was a turn for the books.

"Sounds intriguing. I can get away around five. Will that do?"

"Perfect. I'll see you then."

She was about to chastise him for not calling her by her first name, but then thought better of it. DI McGuinness was a stickler for protocol. She had the feeling that no matter how many times she told him, he'd still insist on Miss Thorne.

By midafternoon, the wind had died down, the temperature had risen into the nineties, and the flurry of pollen had been replaced by swarms of midges. Daisy swatted them out of the way as she made her way across the meadow to the Scout hall. There was a road, but because she'd walked to work and it was such a brilliant day, she didn't want to go home first to get her car. Besides, nothing in Edgemead took that long to get to on foot.

Fifteen minutes later and dripping in perspiration, she was regretting her decision.

DI McGuinness sat outside at a low wooden table with two connected benches on either side waiting for her. It had obviously been designed for children and made his legs look ridiculously long. "Please, sit down." He motioned to the opposite bench. "We can talk out here. The barn is sweltering."

There were two bottles of water in front of him. He passed one to her.

Daisy flopped down and gratefully took a sip. She felt as if she were melting. Her clothes were sticking to her and perspiration was running down her cleavage. She pulled her blouse away from her clammy skin and wished she had a moment to compose herself.

"Nice to see you, Inspector. How is the investigation going?"

He shrugged. "Slowly but surely. I wanted to ask what you know about Collin Harrison. What kind of man is he?"

She cut to the chase. "You mean is he capable of murdering his wife?"

He inclined his head.

Daisy thought for a moment. Did he fit the profile of a killer?

"I think he genuinely loved Serena when they got married, so he's capable of feeling deep emotions and, of course, he's having an affair, so he has normal masculine desires. . . . "

He was watching her closely.

"But Serena was a difficult woman, particularly in the last few years. She had a drinking problem, as you know, which made her mood swings even more violent than usual. She had a terrible temper. One minute she could be charming, the next a complete harridan, screaming at Collin or anyone else who was in the firing range. I heard they had some fantastic rows, but as far as I know, he never abused her in any way, so he can control himself and his temper, and he doesn't get physically aggressive."

"So, you don't think he could have done it?"

"He doesn't really fit the profile, does he? You'd know more about this sort of thing than me." Her course had only just begun covering criminal profiling.

"I'm asking for a character reference, not a psychological profile."

"Oh, well in that case, I can tell you he was very controlled; appearances mattered to him. He didn't come from money, but worked his way up to the successful man he is today."

"So, he wouldn't have wanted to damage his image?"

"No, it's not likely; however, he did have a narcissistic side."

At his inquisitive look, she explained. "Collin was the type of guy who'd wine and dine you if he thought you had something to offer, and then dump you just as fast if something better came up. I've seen it happen. He befriended Colonel Snodgrass because he wanted to poke around his World War Two attic, but when he realized there was nothing of value, he didn't bother to contact him again. The poor colonel felt very used."

"He's an art dealer, I gather?"

"Yes, and a very good one by all accounts. He loves

hunting down old masterpieces, then selling them for obscene amounts of money to private buyers. He can sniff out a valuable piece of art a mile away, a bit like a bloodhound. His gallery is in Mayfair."

McGuinness wrapped his big hands around his water bottle. "I've been to his gallery. They haven't seen him since Saturday."

"The night Serena died. And he's not in the Bahamas?"

McGuinness gave her a strange look. "No, he didn't get on the flight, as I think you well know."

Daisy smiled. "I have a friend who works at Heathrow."

"Of course you do." McGuinness sighed and ran a hand through his hair. It was damp at the temples and the moisture from the water bottle made it stand up in messy spikes. "Why would he pretend to go away?"

Daisy gnawed her lower lip, then said, "There was some talk about an affair with an air stewardess. Violeta, the housekeeper, said that's what he and Serena had been arguing about before he walked out. He was leaving her."

McGuinness slammed his hand down on the table, making Daisy jump. "Why am I only hearing about this now?"

Daisy, who didn't like surprises, glared at him. "Violeta was in shock when you questioned her before, and if you don't mind me saying, you aren't the most approachable of men."

"You don't think I'm approachable?" He glared back at her.

It was a standoff. Her blue eyes locked with his gray ones. "No, I don't. While that steely glare no doubt works to intimidate suspects, it doesn't work too well on witnesses or harmless locals who might have inside information."

"Or you, quite clearly."

She chuckled, easing the tension. "I don't intimidate easily."

"Point taken." His broad shoulders unfurled as he leaned back on the bench. "So, how do you suggest I get the locals to open up to me?"

She pursed her lips. "Well, you could smile more, that might be a good start, and stop glaring at everyone as if they're a suspect."

He folded his arms across his chest and fixed his gaze on her.

"Kinda like now," she said pointedly.

He sighed and turned his head to study a small herd of cows grazing in the meadow. "You're asking me to be someone I'm not."

"That's why you should work with me. I know everyone involved in the case, and they open up to me. I can find out anything you need to know." She leaned forward across the table and smiled coquettishly. "You should use me more. It will be to your advantage."

His eyes narrowed as he gazed at her contemplatively. "Okay, you win, Miss Thorne. Very well played. I admit, your local knowledge would be an advantage in this case. But I have to warn you, if you find anything important, you must let me know, because without properly documented witness statements, we won't be able to prosecute."

"I know the rules, Inspector. My grandfather was a detective."

"Yes, well, times have changed a bit since his day," he said gruffly. "There's a procedure now, and trust me, criminals will do whatever they can to find a loophole. Our case has to be watertight."

Daisy nodded. "I understand, and please, if we're going to be working together, do you think you might call me Daisy? I really hate Miss Thorne."

"Okay, Daisy, and you may as well call me Paul."

She grinned. "Okay, Paul. Well, now that we've cleared that up, there are a few things I should tell you."

He frowned. "Like what?"

"About Sergio, Tatiana's Polish boyfriend, for starters, and then I'll tell you what I know about Pepe's rheumatism. I'm not sure if it's relevant or not, but it's better that you know."

Paul listened in amazement as Daisy explained how she'd questioned Sergio at the bar and discovered he hadn't been home on Saturday night. "He didn't know anything about the steak, you see." She turned her hands palms up on the table. "They both lied."

When she got to Pepe's visit to the doctor, he scratched his chin, which was beginning to show signs of a five-o'clock shadow. "He's an old man. Do you really think he'd be capable of something like this?"

Daisy shook her head. "No, to be honest, I don't. Violeta is younger than Pepe, but even so, I can't imagine them plotting to steal the Modigliani, let alone killing Serena. Besides, according to them, they were at their daughter's house on Saturday night. I just thought I ought to mention it because it does give them a motive."

"I'll check up on their alibi, but their fingerprints are likely to be all over the house."

"Hers, but not his." Pepe hardly ever ventured into the house itself, apart from the kitchen. "I suppose you checked the balustrade?"

He gave her a look that said, *what kind of policeman do you think I am?*

"Sorry." Daisy grimaced. "What about the whiskey bottle?"

He swatted a couple of midges out of the way. "We're still waiting on forensics to get back to us on that, but even if we did find her prints on it, it would be circumstantial."

"So you'd need a confession." It was more a statement than a question.

"Preferably, yes." He studied her across the table. "Or something definite that would stand up in court."

"What about Sergio?" she asked, wiping a bead of sweat from her forehead.

"I'll have him brought in for questioning," McGuinness acknowledged, then his face relaxed slightly. "My intimidating glare might come in useful with him."

Daisy laughed. "I'll leave you to it. I've got to get home. Floria and her father are coming around for dinner."

"Floria's father?"

"Yes, Sir Ranulph; that's Serena's first husband. He flew back from the south of France as soon as Floria told him the news. I expect he'll be at the memorial service, along with Serena's other exes and countless lovers." She shook her head. "It's a bit of a circus."

"What do you know about the other ex-husbands?"

"Not a lot. I only know Sir Ranulph because Floria and I stayed with him in the south of France last summer. He's got a lovely, crumbling mansion out there. Not short of cash, that's for sure. He was quite a bit older than Serena, more like a father figure than a husband, but perhaps that's what she needed at the time. He got her career going. Then there's Hubert, Serena's second hubby. I have no idea how Serena didn't notice he was gay before they were married, but he's a sweetie—wouldn't hurt a fly. Niall is the Irish charmer, always has a glamorous woman on his arm, but he did fall hard for Serena. She divorced him, but it was amicable, or so I'm told. Then she met Collin, but by that stage she was drinking heavily, and I think things turned south pretty quickly."

"You seem to know the family pretty well." He'd been listening hard while she was talking but hadn't made a single note.

"I've been friends with Floria for a long time. Every year Serena hosted these glamorous garden parties—that Floria organized, by the way—so I've met her exes several times. Last year's was particularly interesting. Collin caught Serena making out with a young Russian musician called Vladimir Kustov and went berserk. He threatened to leave her then, but he didn't. Luckily, it was at the end of the party, so not many of the guests were still there, and the ones who were, were too sozzled to remember any-thing clearly." She laughed, then her face fell. "Floria was extremely upset, though, because Serena was beastly to her when she tried to calm things down." She shook her head. "She really wasn't a very nice woman, you know."

Paul raised an eyebrow. "So I've been told. It doesn't excuse what happened, though. Her killer still needs to be brought to justice."

"Oh, of course. I didn't mean that. It's just that she in-flicted so much pain on the people closest to her, and she was desperately unhappy herself. It's tragic, really."

There was a pause as Daisy reflected on her words. Poor Floria; but at least something good had come out of it. Hopefully, her three half sisters would make up for

Serena's nastiness and disinterest over the years. Her friend would have a proper family at last.

Paul looked at his watch, then threw his long legs over the bench and stood up. "Thanks for coming down here, Daisy. You've given me a much clearer picture of all the players in this little drama."

She smiled. "I'm only too happy to help. See you tomorrow, Paul." And she left him standing there, staring after her, as she wove her way back through the meadow toward her house.

Chapter Eight

Daisy had just set the table when Floria arrived with an enormous bunch of white roses in one arm and her father gripping precariously to the other. Sir Ranulph had aged since Daisy had last seen him at Serena's garden party back in May. It was only two months ago, but his hair was now completely white and his face was weary and lined despite his Mediterranean tan, or perhaps because of it. His eyes, however, still sparkled with the same blue intensity as his daughter's.

"Daisy, it's so nice to see you." He leaned forward on his cane and kissed her on both cheeks. He smelled of Eau Savage and stale cigars.

"Likewise, Sir Ranulph. Please, come in and make yourself comfortable. These are gorgeous, Floria." She took the roses into the kitchen to put in a blue-green glass vase—one of her favorites—while Floria led her father into the living room area. Once seated, the retired music producer put his cane aside and muttered, "This damn thing isn't as good as my last one. Some bugger swiped it from a restaurant in Nice last week."

"What a shame." Daisy came back with a bottle of red.

She poured everyone a glass and the three of them sat and chatted while the salmon baked in the oven.

"Did you know about Serena's other daughters?" Daisy had been dying to ask the question since Floria's father had arrived.

Sir Ranulph shook his head. "No, it came as quite a shock. I thought I knew everything about Floria's mother when we got married, but she didn't say a word about any illegitimate children. Not in all the years we were married. I had no idea."

"It's a big secret to keep," muttered Daisy. "One daughter would be hard to hide, but three . . .?"

Sir Ranulph stared into his wine. "She was an incredibly focused woman and she had a way of blocking out things that didn't agree with her vision. To her, they simply wouldn't have existed."

"I've been doing some more Googling," Floria said, changing the subject. "It seems my half sisters, apart from being hugely talented, also have fairly colorful histories."

"Definitely related, then." Daisy laughed. Floria had been rather wild in the days before she'd met James and, consequently, had a reputation as quite the party girl, not unlike her mother.

"Remember I mentioned Mimi, the Australian one, was in a band called Toxic Phonix . . ."

"Was?" Daisy preempted her.

"I'm getting there." Floria grinned. "And this is the good part. A few weeks ago she was sacked for punching the lead singer in the face during a concert. The audience booed her off the stage. Can you believe that?"

Daisy had to laugh. "I can't wait to meet her."

Sir Ranulph shook his head. "That's no way for a singer to behave."

"Then there's her twin, Donna, who lives in Austria. Apparently, they were separated at birth and adopted by two separate sets of parents."

"I didn't know they did that anymore," remarked Daisy. "Split up twins, I mean."

Floria shrugged. "Well, they certainly did in this case. They ended up in opposite corners of the world."

"Did they know about each other?" asked Daisy.

Floria shook her head. "I don't think so. Greg said they both sounded shocked by the news."

Daisy pursed her lips. "What a crazy scenario."

Sir Ranulph nodded in agreement.

Floria got back to her story. "Anyway, Donna, the violinist, seems better behaved. I haven't been able to dig up any dirt on her yet. In fact, I haven't been able to find out much about her at all. She doesn't even have a Facebook profile." She stared at Daisy. "Who's not on social media these days?"

"I'm not," murmured Sir Ranulph, but Floria ignored him and went on.

"Then we come to Carmen, the Spanish one. Isn't it an ideal name for an opera singer? I wonder if Serena came up with that? Anyway, I've seen a photograph of her singing in Madrid, and she's the spitting image of Mother. You won't believe it, Father. It's creepy."

Sir Ranulph didn't reply. Daisy got the impression he didn't want to be reminded of his late ex-wife, especially a younger, more beautiful version, like Serena had been when they'd first met.

"She's also a model," added Floria, "but then, she is

very striking and singing rarely pays the bills until you're famous. At work, singers and musicians come in all the time begging for an advance on their royalties. They're desperate, hoping to strike it lucky with their next album, but it hardly ever happens."

Floria would know. Her job as an executive's assistant at the production company included lots of running around pacifying temperamental musicians.

Sir Ranulph patted his daughter's hand. "I'm sure none of them are as kind or as pretty as my blond, blue-eyed girl."

Floria smiled. "Thank goodness I have you, Papa."

"I'd do anything for you, you know that, Floria."

She got up and gave him a hug.

"When is the funeral?" asked Sir Ranulph as they moved to the dining room table. Daisy's cottage was open-plan, with the dining room almost an extension of the kitchen, separated by a shiny, white bar counter. Daisy loved the layout because when she was in the kitchen preparing food or drinks, she could still talk to her guests in the seating area.

"It's a memorial service, Father, and it'll be on Friday." Floria glanced at Daisy. "Your DI McGuinness said they'd release the body next week so we can bury her properly."

Sir Ranulph cringed. "I can't bear to think of her like that. Do you know what happened? The police wouldn't tell me much, other than that she was killed over a stolen painting. The Modigliani, was it?"

Daisy glanced at Floria. "I'll fetch the salmon."

Floria pulled out his chair and he sat down. Daisy could hear them from the kitchen.

"It appears Mother interrupted the burglar and he hit

her over the head. Then she lost her balance and fell—or was pushed—over the balustrade. She'd been drinking heavily, which wouldn't have helped."

The old man's voice trembled. "Poor woman. I admit there was no love lost between us at the end, but I wouldn't have wished that on anyone. Also, Collin must be distraught over the missing Modigliani. He acquired that for Serena, if I remember correctly?"

Floria didn't immediately reply. Daisy saved her from having to explain that Collin had gone missing by carrying in the baked salmon surrounded by an assortment of roasted vegetables on a large tray.

"Here, let me help you with that." Floria jumped up to clear some space. "It looks delicious, Daisy, and perfect for this balmy weather."

"That's what I thought." She placed the tray on the table and proceeded to dish up.

"Daisy has hit it off with DI McGuinness," Floria told her father, a sly grin on her face. "I must admit, he is rather dishy if you like the strong, silent type."

Daisy didn't deny it. "He's agreed to let me help him."

"With the investigation?" Sir Ranulph paused with his fork halfway to his mouth. "Isn't that dangerous, Daisy?"

"No, not at all. I hear things in the salon; my customers talk to me. I promised the inspector that if I heard anything important, I'd feed it back to him, that's all. I'm not going to go around questioning suspects or anything like that."

"I thought that's exactly what you were doing," mumbled Floria, her mouth full.

Daisy shot her a warning glance.

"Well, just be careful, my dear. There are a lot of crazies out there."

Later, when Sir Ranulph was settled with a brandy in the living room, Classic FM playing gently in the background, Daisy asked Floria to help her load the dishwasher.

Once safely in the kitchen and out of earshot, she asked her friend about Serena's ex-husbands.

Floria's eyes grew wide. "They're not under suspicion, surely? Father is harmless, as you know, and neither Niall nor Hubert are that hard up."

"I suppose Paul has to rule them out."

"Paul?" Floria raised an eyebrow. "So, we're on a first name basis now, are we?"

Daisy gave her a look and continued. "As I was saying, all three of them knew about the painting and how valuable it was." All three of their names had been on his whiteboard.

Floria thought for a moment. "Well, you can tell *Paul*," she emphasized the name, "that Niall is on a ranch in Argentina looking at a young filly he thinks has potential, and Hubert is firmly ensconced with his partner, Lucian, at their house in Kent. I can give you their contact numbers. I spoke to both of them yesterday to tell them Mother had died. I thought it better coming from me than the press."

"That would be great." She smiled at her friend. "And how are you holding up? We haven't had a moment to talk about what happened with James."

Floria had been with James for almost a year, and Daisy knew how serious she'd been about him.

Her friend's face dropped. "He was really hurtful, Dais.

I know he's ambitious and all, but I was shocked by his callousness."

They perched on the kitchen countertop.

"Tell me what happened."

"We went to Posticino's for dinner. James said he had something he wanted to talk to me about. For a minute there I thought he might be proposing." She gave a self-deprecating laugh. "Silly me, right?"

Daisy smiled sympathetically.

"But what he actually wanted to talk about was ending our relationship. Now he's an MP, he can't be seen with a party girl like me." She rolled her eyes. "His words, not mine. He mentioned the photograph in *The Star* and said publicity like that was bad for his image, and he was under pressure from his political peers to end our relationship."

Her eyes filled with tears. "I thought I meant more to him than that."

Daisy gave her a hug. "I'm so sorry, Flo. He doesn't deserve you. He should have defended you to his peers, not agreed to break up with you. The man has no back-bone."

Floria sniffed. "It's true. He never had any backbone, he hated to offend anyone, particularly his superiors."

James was on a fast-track to a high-profile political career, and he wouldn't do anything to jeopardize that. Daisy considered herself a good judge of character, and she'd pegged James for a self-centered, brown-nosing egotist the minute she'd met him, but she also knew from personal experience that nothing she said would make Floria feel any better. The heart takes time to mend, and even though James had been far too stuck-up and stuffy for a free spirit like Floria, it still hurt and would for some time.

"I suppose it's better I found out now than years down the line." At least Floria was thinking rationally.

"You're absolutely right. You wouldn't want to be tied to a man like that. I always thought he had a nasty streak."

"You did, I know, but you were always too polite to tell me. I think I sensed it myself, if I'm honest, but I was in denial. He was such a catch."

"You're more of a catch," Daisy said loyally, and she meant it. Floria was well-connected, came from a wealthy family, had an excellent education and was a vivacious, fun-loving person to boot. What man wouldn't want to be with a girl like that?

"Thanks, honey. I know he wasn't right for me, but I can't help feeling sad it's all over. Coming to terms with Mother's death, finding out about my sisters—it's all been so overwhelming. It's at times like this when I need a strong shoulder to cry on." A single tear escaped and ran down her cheek.

"You have me and your father," Daisy said, climbing off the countertop and starting to load the dirty plates into the dishwasher. "And soon you'll have your three sisters too. You don't need stuffy, old James. He didn't have very good shoulders anyway."

Floria laughed despite her tears. "No, they were nowhere near broad enough, not like your police detective." The laughter died in her throat. "James hasn't even called to commiserate. He must have heard by now; it's been all over the news. He's probably thanking his lucky stars he dumped me before Mother's death hit the media."

"In that case, very good riddance," muttered Daisy, slotting the last of the plates into the dishwasher.

"I know, I keep telling myself that, but it still hurts."

"Of course it does. These things take time to get over. It took me months to get over Tim."

"Tim was different. He just up and left. Apart from the heartbreak, you had the added worry of not knowing what had become of him. You were beside yourself. At least I know James is still alive and kicking, even if it is in the House of Commons."

Daisy bit her lip. Why had she brought up Tim? Even after two years, talking about him still made her uncomfortable. She knew it shouldn't; it had been so long ago. If she was honest, she put it down to the humiliation of being abandoned. Not only had it destroyed her self-confidence, but she'd been embarrassed that he'd left her high and dry without so much as a goodbye. Worse still, the whole village knew about it. If there was one thing she hated more than being dumped, it was being pitied. So she'd pasted a smile on her face and continued like nothing had happened.

"Oh, it was ending anyway," she'd said to customers who'd commiserated with her.

"We'd grown apart" was her standard response to people who stopped her in the street to say how sorry they were. Truth be told, none of those things were true. The evening before Tim had left, they'd gone for a stroll along the river, held hands and kissed under the weeping willows. That night they'd made love and he'd been as tender and loving as ever. Looking back, perhaps even more so than usual. She'd had absolutely no inkling that he was going to walk out of her life the very next day.

Still, it had happened, and she, who prided herself on being a good judge of character, hadn't seen it coming. She flushed, the shame still getting the better of her. "It's true, but it was obvious he wanted out. He'd packed his stuff and taken the car. It's not like he was kidnapped or anything. It just took a while for the reality to sink in."

"Still, a nasty way to leave someone. Even a letter or a text would have been better. Celebs break up via text message all the time. It's quite the done thing nowadays."

"So I've heard." She didn't want to talk about Tim anymore. The pain had subsided and most people had forgotten about him, but she'd have to live with the private humiliation for the rest of her life.

Floria was saying, "I know it sounds strange, but I'm grateful that I have Mother's memorial to arrange. It will be a welcome distraction."

Daisy knew what she meant. Floria loved organizing events, particularly parties, and was exceptionally good at it. Every detail was taken care of from the invitations and venue to the catering and decorations. She had organized every one of Serena's garden parties for as far back as Daisy could remember, and there must have been over a hundred guests at the last one.

A memorial service was a different affair, but given Serena's popularity and massive fan base, Floria would have her work cut out for her; but if nothing else, it would take her mind off James.

Chapter Nine

"I was thinking about Collin," Daisy said to Floria, who arrived at Ooh La La with a tray of lattes from Costa Coffee in Esher. The team fell on them in ecstasy.

"You mean where he's hiding?" Floria asked.

"He's probably shacked up with his air stewardess," remarked Krish with foam on his upper lip. Asa gestured for him to wipe it off.

"Who would know who she is?" asked Daisy thoughtfully. "Who would he tell? If we could track her down, we might be able to locate him."

"Unless he's left the country," interjected Penny.

"Brompton Court is still out of bounds or we could search his study for clues." Floria raised her eyebrows over her coffee. "He might have a calendar or diary stashed away."

"Perhaps we still can." Daisy tapped her middle finger against her cup. "And there's also his office at the gallery."

"Oh, his assistant, Bronwyn, takes care of everything. She practically runs the place."

At Daisy's pursed lips she added, "But I'm sure I could convince her to let us look around."

"I'm going to need you guys to hold down the fort this afternoon," Daisy told her team, all of whom nodded earnestly. "While we do a bit of snooping. Are you up for it, Flo?"

"Try keeping me away." Floria's eyes sparkled.

"Don't worry about a thing." Krish took an overexcited gulp of his coffee and yelped as it burned his tongue. "We've got it all under control."

Brompton Court stood silent and golden against a backdrop of cloudless blue sky. Daisy drove up the winding driveway past the mellow woods at the bottom of the garden, past the beautifully landscaped lawns, the duck pond and the stone nymph fountain, before finally coming to a stop outside the house. It was only when they got close that the police tape across the front entrance became visible.

"It still takes my breath away," murmured Floria, staring up at the symmetrical façade with its four pillars on the portico shimmering in the afternoon sun.

"It is spectacular," Daisy agreed. Built on a hill, the mansion offered stunning views in all directions, but from outside at ground level, looking up, it was majestic.

A young, uniformed police officer who'd been stationed outside the property approached them. "I'm sorry, ma'am. This property is off-limits."

"I'm Dame Serena Levanté's daughter and I live here." Floria was stretching the truth, although Daisy supposed it had been true at one point. "I've got to fetch a few personal items. I didn't pack properly after the incident. I was too upset."

The police officer looked dubious. "I'm under strict orders not to let anyone in."

"Does that include immediate family?" She flashed her cobalt-blue eyes at him, almost the same color as the sky, and Daisy saw him wilt.

They were in.

Floria gave him a grateful smile and pulled out her key. "I promise we won't be long."

"And we won't disturb anything," Daisy added, slipping in after her friend.

"That was very well done," she whispered as they side-skirted the place where Serena had died, marked by a yellow placard, and inched their way up the grand staircase.

Serena's portrait smiled down enigmatically on them as they crossed the landing. Daisy stopped beneath it and stared up. "You know who killed you, don't you?" she whispered.

"She took that secret with her to the grave," Floria replied, suppressing a shiver. "But then, she was good at that."

Collin's study was at the end of a passageway on the west side of the house. It was a spacious room, luxuriously decorated with wood paneling and built-in shelves filled with books on art and design. The floor was carpeted and partially covered by a Persian rug. Collin's work desk was antique—probably Victorian—upon which lay an open diary, a letter opener with a solid silver handle and a small pile of unopened mail.

Daisy, who'd never been in the study before, paused to admire the view from behind the French doors that led out to a small balcony. She could see the emerald-green lawns undulating down to the woods, the pond, complete with ducks swimming in it and the stone water nymph that insisted on spurting merrily despite the ominous events that had occurred under her very nose.

Floria, her back to Daisy, gazed in the opposite direction at an empty space on the wall behind the desk. "That's where the Modigliani was."

Daisy whipped around. The wallpaper was darker where the painting had hung. Before the Modigliani, there had no doubt been another priceless work of art in its place.

"Collin will be devastated," Floria whispered, touching the space where it should have been.

"Unless he took it." Daisy approached the desk. "Let's look for anything that might give us a clue as to who he was seeing, although I tend to agree with you: If he was having an affair, he would want to keep it from Serena, in which case we may have more luck at the gallery."

"It's worth checking anyway," said Floria. "I'll take the drawers on the right, you take the left."

So, together they searched through what was mostly bills and invoices, although they did find the provenances belonging to some of the more valuable paintings Serena and Collin kept in the mansion, covered in protective plastic sleeves. Daisy recognized the custodian documentation for the Stubbs, the little Pissarro and, of course, the missing Modigliani.

Next, she picked up a worn, leather-bound notebook and flicked through it. "I've found a notebook detailing what looks like potential sellers." Her eyes widened. "This is a treasure trove of information. It contains the details of all his contacts from all over Europe. I know a few art dealers who would give their eyeteeth to get their hands on this. I'm surprised it's not under lock and key."

Floria tutted. "There's a pile here too, going back donkey's years. These should really be in a safe."

"Anything that could indicate where he's been meeting his mystery woman?" Daisy asked, carefully setting the notebook back in the drawer where she'd found it.

"Nothing on my side." Floria closed the last drawer and sighed. "It was a long shot."

"There's a receipt here from Liberty," remarked Daisy, taking it out of a folder filled with similar receipts. "The perfumery. Now that *is* interesting."

"What did he buy?"

"Christian Dior Hypnotic Poison."

"So it is a gift for his lover, but it doesn't tell us any more about her other than she's got expensive taste." Floria sat in the leather armchair in front of the desk and fiddled with the letter opener. "I wonder who she is."

"Bernadette, apparently." Daisy perched on the desk. The forensic team had already dusted the place for finger-prints, so she didn't think there'd be any harm in them having a poke around. "Didn't Violeta say Collin met her on a flight to Paris?"

"Yes, that's right," Floria confirmed.

Daisy bit her lip thoughtfully. "So can we assume she's French? Bernadette is a French name."

"That would explain why nobody has located him," said Floria. "If he's hiding out in France, he might not even be aware Mother is dead."

"It would be in the French papers," Daisy pointed out. "But he might not have seen them."

"Do you think your friend could check the BA flights to Paris on Saturday night?"

"I'll ask her." Daisy whipped out her phone and sent a text message to Asa.

"We'd better get out of here before that policeman reports us," said Floria, getting up. She cast her eyes over the desk to make sure it was as they'd left it.

Daisy, who'd been pacing the room, glanced out of the window.

"Too late," she murmured. "DI McGuinness has arrived and he doesn't look happy."

Floria grimaced. "I'd better get some personal items from my old room; otherwise they'll be suspicious."

"Don't bother." Daisy flicked the receipt. "We have leverage. The inspector will know we were here to snoop anyway."

They raced downstairs and were met by a stony-faced DI McGuinness in the entrance hall.

"You do realize this is a crime scene," he barked, his brow furrowed. He looked quite intimidating.

Floria glanced nervously at Daisy, who flashed him her best smile. "I'm sorry, Paul, but we were looking for information on Collin's mystery lover. We thought it might help us locate him."

His eyes flickered as he studied her. There was a long pause, but eventually he said, "And did you?"

"We found a receipt from Liberty, which we think was a gift." She handed it to him. "It's for expensive French perfume."

"Mother only wears Chanel," Floria added helpfully.

"What does this tell us?" His gaze moved from Daisy to Floria and back again.

"We think he's in France." Daisy nodded toward the receipt. "Violeta said he met her on a flight to Paris, and he's bought her French perfume."

"And her name is Bernadette," Floria reminded him.

"I bet if you check, you'll find he took a flight to France the night of Serena's death and not the Bahamas, like we thought." Daisy hoped she was right. If it were true, it would rule out Serena's latest husband as a suspect. The Bahamas was just a trick to throw Serena off the scent.

"I will check."

DI McGuinness shepherded them out the front door and gestured to the red-faced police officer to lock it.

"I've also got the mobile phone numbers for Sir Ranulph Haines, Niall Barclay and Hubert Laughton, Serena's exes." Daisy fished in her handbag for the paper on which she'd written them down and handed it to DI McGuinness. He took it and studied the names.

"Serena didn't take her first husband's surname?"

"No, she didn't," Floria explained. "Her audiences knew her as Levanté, so she kept it."

He nodded and pocketed the list.

"My father is staying with me until you allow us back into Brompton Court," Floria added.

"You can move back in on Thursday," he confirmed. "I hope that gives you enough time to prepare for the reception?"

Daisy was surprised the gruff inspector had considered the memorial preparations. Floria, on the other hand, had gone into party-planning mode. "Yes, although with only a day to spare, I'll have to hire cleaners to get the place shipshape. Violeta won't be able to cope by herself. Many of the overseas guests will stay the night, so we have to get the bedrooms sorted."

Daisy estimated there were about fifteen bedrooms at Brompton Court, most of which were rarely used. Dame Serena and Collin had separate rooms, both on the west side of the house near Collin's study and the section of the landing where Serena had fallen to her death. The few times Daisy had stayed over, she'd been put up in one of the many guest rooms in the east wing, next to Floria's old bedroom. Floria had explained that when she was young, the nanny had occupied that room. Serena's schedule was such that the opera diva hadn't the time or inclination to tend to Floria's needs, and so a full-time nanny was always in residence.

"I believe the reading of the will is to take place after the reception on Friday?" DI McGuinness said. It was more of a statement than a question, though.

Floria nodded. "Yes, Greg thought it would be most appropriate because my sisters will be here by then."

Daisy saw a flush steal into her friend's cheeks. Every time her sisters were mentioned, Floria practically sizzled with excitement. It was going to be a very emotional weekend. Hundreds were coming to the memorial service, although only Serena's closest friends—if she had such a thing—had been invited to the reception.

"Will you let us know what you find out about Collin?" Daisy reached into her pocket for her car keys. If they wanted to get to Mayfair before five o'clock, when the gallery shut, they'd better get a move on. Her aim was to park at the station and catch the train into Waterloo. From there they'd navigate by tube to the gallery.

DI McGuinness met her gaze. "Of course."

Daisy smiled her thanks, then got into the car with Floria and they drove down the meandering driveway leaving Brompton Court shimmering in the afternoon sun behind them.

Chapter Ten

Bronwyn, Collin's meticulous personal assistant, was tidying up the gallery after a busy day when Daisy and Floria arrived. Floria explained that they urgently needed to locate Collin, and could they have a look in his office to see if there was anything that might tell them where he was?

"Absolutely not," said Bronwyn, aghast. "I can't let you look in Mr. Harrison's office. He'd kill me."

Daisy could see she wouldn't budge, so she tried a different angle. "Bronwyn, do you have access to Collin's diary? Perhaps you can tell us if he had anything planned or booked this week?"

The PA gnawed her lower lip, then made a decision. "Okay, sure. I guess there's no harm in that." She sat down in front of her computer and opened Outlook. Her eyes scrolled across, and then down the screen. "No, he had nothing booked until Thursday; that's tomorrow."

Daisy raised her eyebrows. "So it's quite likely he could have gone away for a few days?"

"He's always off on business trips and he never tells me where he's going. Sometimes I get a phone call from somewhere abroad, canceling his appointments for the next few days, and other times, like now, the calendar is empty until he's due back."

"So this is normal for him?" Collin had planned to be away, then.

His PA nodded. "Yes, like I told the police the other day, he often does this. It's nothing out of the ordinary."

"So you're not worried he's gone missing or anything?"

"God, no." She looked alarmed. "Should I be?"

"Oh, no," Daisy rushed to reassure her. "We're just trying to ascertain if this is his normal pattern, that's all. If so—and by the sounds of things it is—there's nothing to worry about."

Bronwyn's shoulders sank and she exhaled, visibly relieved.

"Right, thank you, Bronwyn," Daisy said. "You've been really helpful."

She smiled, somewhat hesitantly. Daisy got the impression she didn't get much in the way of praise. "I don't know if you're interested, but Floria and I were going to have drinks and a light supper at the Arts Club. You could join us, if you're free?"

The Arts Club was an exclusive members' club situated a stone's throw from the gallery. It sported five floors of luxury, including a sushi restaurant, an oyster bar, a brasserie and a sunny terrace, and in the evenings you could listen to jazz or soul in the basement. Floria, who worked in Mayfair, used it for relaxed meetings with musicians her boss wanted to impress and ultimately sign.

"They have the best sushi," Floria added, catching on.

"Thank you, but I have to lock up at five." Her voice was filled with disappointment.

"It's okay, it's only half an hour. We'll wait." Daisy smiled at her. "It's been a while since I've been here. I'd like to have a look around."

"Well, okay. If you're sure you don't mind?"

"Not at all," Daisy said firmly. "The more the merrier. You finish up and then we'll get going. I'm looking forward to a glass of bubbly."

Bronwyn whizzed around, positioning scatter cushions and polishing mirrors, then she swept the floors and, finally, gathered up all the cups on her desk. "I'll just wash these up and then we can go," she called before dashing off to the kitchen.

"Keep an eye out," whispered Daisy as she slunk off toward Collin's office. Luckily, the glass door was unlocked; his office was adjacent to Bronwyn's, and the PA had, no doubt, been in and out during the day.

Wasting no time, she attacked the desk, pulling out draws and leafing through the contents in rapid succession. She found nothing frivolous, only work-related stuff. She did notice, however, his laptop was missing. It hadn't been in his study at Brompton Court either, which meant he must have it with him.

She heard Floria whistle gently. Bronwyn was coming back. Taking one last look around, Daisy spotted the wastebasket. It had a few scraps of paper in it. Out of time, she grabbed them and stuffed them into her handbag before darting out of the office and into Bronwyn's. But she was too late. The secretary was already outside the door. In a panic, she looked around for somewhere to hide; then she heard Floria say, "Bronwyn, I don't remember the Anthony van Dyck. When did Collin acquire it?"

The sound of retreating footsteps told Daisy that Floria

had led Bronwyn off into the other room, giving her a precious few minutes. With relief, she darted out of the office and went to join them. "That's better; I was bursting."

Bronwyn shut down her computer, locked the door to Collin's office and then her own. Daisy had to admit she was very thorough. She checked all the locks afterward, and ushered them out before setting the burglar alarm, after which she vacated the gallery herself. The front door had two bolts that she locked using unusually shaped keys. She then activated the solid aluminum security door via a remote control attached to her key ring. "You can't be too careful with those old masters and impressionist paintings inside. Criminals these days are so technically advanced."

Not surprisingly, The Arts Club was bustling thanks to the fine weather. They got a table outside on the terrace and ordered a bottle of prosecco.

Bronwyn, who couldn't stop looking around in case she spotted someone famous, asked when the funeral was.

"We're having a memorial service on Friday," Floria told her. "I've announced it in the national press, although I'm keeping the reception strictly private, otherwise it'll be mayhem." I remember last time Serena hosted an open house, we had to call the police to remove the lingering guests at about four in the morning, and then we still found couples sleeping it off in the woods the next day.

Once they were onto their second glass and everybody's mood had lifted, Daisy turned to Bronwyn and asked, "Did you know Collin was having an affair?"

The PA spluttered on her prosecco. "What? No, I had no idea."

Daisy leaned forward, taking her into her confidence. "Apparently, he told Serena as much the day she died. The poor woman was devastated, as you can imagine."

"The housekeeper found her bawling her eyes out," Floria divulged. Her voice dropped to a whisper. "But please don't tell anyone. I wouldn't want the press to get wind of it." That much was true. Although Serena's reputation of late couldn't get much worse, they didn't want the world to know she'd been dumped by her fourth husband the day she was murdered.

Bronwyn's eyes were out on stalks. "I swear I didn't know. He didn't say anything to me."

"Are you sure? He didn't ask for restaurant recommendations or to book any romantic getaways for two?"

"Suggestions for French perfume?" cut in Floria.

"No, nothing like that." Her brow creased in concentration, then she said, "But he did ask me a strange question the other day."

"Oh, what was that?" Daisy perked up.

"He asked me if I'd ever been to Lourmarin. It's a small village in the south of France. I only know it because we used to go to Avignon on holiday when I was a child, and it was close by. I said I had and it was very picturesque, but we left it at that. Do you think that's where he is?" She stared at them with wide eyes.

"I don't know." Daisy met Floria's gaze over Bronwyn's head. "He could be shacked up there with his mistress. It's a pity we don't have the name of a guesthouse or some way of contacting him."

"He might not even know Mother's dead." Floria deliberately choked on the words.

"Have you tried his mobile?" Bronwyn asked. They both nodded.

"What about his work phone?"

They stared at her. "You mean he has a second phone?"

"Oh yes, for work contacts. Here, I'll give you the number."

She took out her mobile and scrolled through it for a few seconds. "Ah, here we go."

She read off the number, which Floria immediately dialed. Daisy found she was holding her breath. If he was having an affair, it would make sense he had a second phone, and probably an untraceable one too.

"It rang, but went to voice mail," said Floria, disappointed.

Daisy picked up her glass and downed what was left in it. But it wasn't switched off, which meant Paul might be able to trace it. Jubilant, she grinned at her companions. "Shall we order? I'm starving."

Chapter Eleven

DI McGuinness was waiting for her when she got home. The night was balmy, and he was sitting in his car with the door open, music playing softly on the radio.

"Hello, Paul," she said as she approached from the rear. "To what do I owe the pleasure?"

As he climbed out of the car, Daisy was struck by how tired he looked. His eyes had purple circles beneath them and his five-o'clock shadow was now dark stubble that covered most of his jaw and neck. Even the soft Irish lilt that earlier had been barely noticeable was more pronounced. "I came to tell you that we arrested Sergio Draganska and Tatiana Shishkova this afternoon."

Daisy gasped. "Because of what I said?"

He nodded. "I thought it warranted further investigation. They are being interviewed under caution by members of my team as we speak, but so far they're both sticking to their story."

"Sergio's tough," Daisy mused. "He's got a healthy disrespect for the law. I wouldn't be surprised if he's been in trouble with the authorities before."

Paul gave her a curious glance. "Funny you should

say that. He did serve a short sentence for petty theft in Poland."

She gave an embarrassed grin. Of course Paul would do background checks on all his suspects.

"How did you guess?"

She shrugged. "I'm good at reading people."

"I'd say."

Daisy opened the door. "Shall we go inside?"

He followed her in.

"Make yourself at home. I'll get us a drink."

"Coffee for me, please. I've got to drive back to Guildford tonight."

"Good idea. I've had far too much prosecco today." She popped on the kettle.

At his raised eyebrow, she elaborated, "Floria and I paid a visit to Collin's gallery after we left you this afternoon. We thought his personal assistant, Bronwyn, might know where he was."

"So you took her out and fed her prosecco?"

Daisy shrugged. "We thought it might help."

"Well, we already questioned her; she didn't know anything. However, we checked with the airlines, and you were right. Collin Harrison flew to Marseilles on Saturday afternoon, which would mean he couldn't have killed Serena on Saturday night."

"So you've crossed him off your suspect list?"

"For now, yes. We'd still like to have a word with him when he gets back. If he gets back."

"I think I can help you with that." Daisy leaned forward on the bar counter. "Collin had a second mobile phone, probably untraceable, which he used for work, but I'm betting his mistress had the number."

Paul stared at her. "A second phone?"

"Yes; it's no secret. Bronwyn gave us the number. Perhaps you can ping him?"

"Damn." He looked thoroughly put out. "Why the hell didn't she give me that information?"

"Perhaps it was the prosecco," Daisy said with a smile.

Paul shook his head. "I should take tips from you."

Daisy grinned at the compliment. When the water had boiled, she made them each a large mug of coffee and walked back into the living room area. "There's more."

He raised an eyebrow and accepted the mug. "I can't wait to hear."

"Collin asked Bronwyn if she'd ever been to a French village called Lourmarin."

Paul scratched his bristly chin. "Lourmarin? I know it. It's near Avignon. But that's a bit of a long shot, isn't it? So what? He may have liked the name of the place."

"But he might have been going there with his lover, the air stewardess. Perhaps he hadn't been before. It's close to Marseilles, isn't it? A short drive in a rented car. Oh, that reminds me. I have his work trash."

"What?" At Paul's confused expression, she ran around the bar counter, picked up her handbag and unceremoniously emptied it onto the coffee table. The contents spilled out and shot in all directions. A lipstick and a tampon rolled off the table and landed at his feet. Paul picked up the items and put them back on the table. He said dryly, "I hope there's a point to all this."

"Getting there." Daisy picked out a crumpled piece of paper and opened it. She held it up in front of him.

"Avis, Marseilles," he read. "This is the car rental company?"

She nodded. "I took it out of his wastebasket when I was in his office today. Then there's this." She unfolded a small Post-it Note and placed it before him. "It's a telephone number. Look, isn't that the French dialing code? I called it earlier, but nobody answered."

"Let me try. There might be an after-hours recording." He pulled out his phone from his pocket and dialed the number. Daisy watched his face as he waited for it to divert to voice mail.

Except it didn't.

His expression turned to one of surprise as someone answered.

"Hello? Yes, with whom am I speaking?"

Daisy held her breath. They were an hour ahead in France, so it would be nearly midnight. That was late for someone to answer, unless it was a residential number.

"Boutique d'art?" Paul switched to French. *"Connaissez-vous* Mr. Harrison? Collin Harrison?"

She listened as Paul interviewed the person on the phone in flawless French. Daisy's French was passable, but nothing like Paul's. She picked up enough to realize that they didn't know, nor had ever heard of Collin.

When he hung up she said, "Your French is *très impressionnant.*"

He grinned. "I paid attention at school."

"Clearly."

She sat opposite him on the sofa, curling her legs underneath her. "So, it was an art store?"

"Yes, in Paris. The woman who answered said they

were hosting an event tonight, which was why they were still open. It seems aboveboard. I suppose Collin could have been passing the number to a contact or something. It is his industry, after all."

Daisy sipped her coffee and studied Paul over her mug. That was more than paying attention in class; he was practically fluent. She'd spent a lot of time in France during school holidays, and he spoke like a local, no hint of an accent. At some point in his life he'd learned to speak the language fluently. The handsome inspector was full of surprises.

"I'll get the techies to ping his phone first thing tomorrow, and if we can get a location, the local French police can contact him."

"According to his diary, he's due back in London tomorrow anyway, but I suppose it's worth a shot."

Paul studied her. "I still don't like you nosing around. It's dangerous, but thank you. This is very useful information."

Daisy picked up her paraphernalia and stuffed it back into her handbag. "We got lucky, that's all. Besides, it looks like Collin's in the clear anyway."

With Collin out of the equation, that left Tatiana and Sergio, or Violeta and Pepe, as their prime suspects. Hopefully, the interrogation would bring something to light. Perhaps it *was* just a burglary gone wrong? Somehow, though, Daisy didn't think things were that simple. She wasn't sure why; it was just a feeling.

"How are you getting on with Serena's other ex-husbands?" she asked, recalling the names on the whiteboard in the makeshift incident room.

"Slowly. We have other lines of inquiry and we're

short-staffed, but we'll get to them." He shook his head. "Four husbands and she wasn't even that old."

"Not to mention the countless lovers," added Daisy with a grin.

"It's a security nightmare," Paul admitted. "Any one of them could have come to the house that night. We're checking their alibis."

"I think you'll find they're all in the clear." Daisy stretched her neck. "None of them had a motive. They're all wealthy in their own right. Besides, Sir Ranulph lives in France, and I think Floria said Niall was away. That leaves Hubert, but he's such an old dear, he wouldn't say boo to a ghost."

"An interesting cast of characters," he mused. "Then there's the illegitimate daughters coming from far and wide to pay their respects."

"At Serena's request?" asked Daisy.

He nodded. "She was quite adamant, according to Mr. Edwards, her solicitor. Apparently, she wanted all the girls to meet."

"A flash of humanity," murmured Daisy, earning herself a surprised look from Paul.

"Oh, Serena wasn't a nice woman," she clarified. "I can say that because it's true. Everybody who knew her had felt the brunt of her temper at one point or another. Poor Floria got the worst of it. I wouldn't have been at all surprised if she'd completely ignored her other daughters and written them off without a penny."

"She may still have planned to do that," surmised Paul. He was thinking about the appointment to change her will.

"It's possible," admitted Daisy. "I'd never take anything for granted where Serena's concerned."

"Thanks for the tip," said Paul.

Daisy stretched her neck. The long day was taking its toll.

"I can see you're tired, so I'll get going." He downed his coffee. Daisy didn't object. She was tired, but she enjoyed his company and didn't want him to go; however, saying so would compromise her, so she didn't reply.

He stood up. "Do you play?" He nodded toward the grand piano in the corner of the room. It had been in her parents' house at one point, but they'd never used it, except as a showpiece, something for guests to tinker with when they came around, so when they'd moved to Spain, she'd expropriated it.

"A little. My mother insisted I take lessons all through school. I hated it back then, but I enjoy playing now. It relaxes me."

"I played the clarinet, but I was so bad at it, I think my mother was secretly relieved when I quit."

Daisy couldn't help laughing. The vision of tall, broad-shouldered Paul playing a clarinet was too incongruous for words.

She got up to show him out. He followed her to the door, his keys jingling in his pocket. A pile of her class books lay on the kitchen countertop. He picked up the top one, titled *Psychology and Violent Crime*, and gave her a quizzical look.

"I'm studying forensic psychology." She felt herself blushing but wasn't sure why. It was a perfectly legitimate area of study. "When I'm qualified I want to help law enforcement agencies profile criminals. It's an interest of mine."

He nodded slowly, a contemplative expression on his face. She had expected ridicule, or at the very least an arched eyebrow, so she was pleasantly surprised.

"You know, nothing much surprises me anymore." He wagged his finger in the air. "But you, Daisy Thorne . . . you surprise me."

She tilted her head to one side. "Is that a good thing?"

She was flirting with him. Good heavens, she hadn't flirted with a man in years, not since Tim left, and after that she hadn't thought it possible she'd be attracted to a man again.

His stormy-gray eyes, which were now much calmer, but no less intense, bore into hers. "Very. Now I'd better be going. I've got a long drive ahead."

Daisy, who had paused with her hand on the doorknob, gave it a hard twist. Cool air rushed in and the moment passed. She stood aside to let him through.

"Thanks for the coffee," he said over his shoulder.

"Any time."

She watched as he climbed into his car and was still watching as he pulled out of the driveway and sped off, his black BMW blending seamlessly into the night.

Chapter Twelve

Floria sank into the comfy leather chair with a soft sigh of delight and lay her head back on the basin. She was having a much-needed cut and blow-dry before the weekend, when she'd be inundated with guests for her mother's memorial service, including her long-lost sisters. It was important she made a good impression.

"The world is going to be watching," she explained to a wide-eyed Asa. "I've already had offers from *Hello!* and *OK!* magazines for an exclusive."

"Heavens," murmured Asa. "Aren't you nervous with all those celebs coming?"

"You get used to it." Floria sighed. "Although Sir Elton's agent rang me yesterday and said he'd be there. He and Mother go way back. That's enough to ensure most of the TV networks will come. It's going to be chaos at the vicarage."

Krish nearly dropped the tray of utensils he was carrying. "Oh my gosh. I'd love to meet him."

"You'll have to make sure you get there early," said Daisy, who'd been listening to their conversation while removing Mrs. Winterbottom's curlers. "The traffic will be gridlocked with limos and Bentleys dropping off their famous passengers."

"Not to mention all the locals who want to pay their respects," added Krish with a pleading look at Daisy.

"Oh, I plan to," said Floria. "The flowers are being delivered first thing, and the vicar wants to revise the service schedule as two of my sisters will be performing."

"Really? That's a wonderful idea. Which two?" asked Daisy, intrigued. She could hear the pride in Floria's voice. Floria's half sisters seemed inordinately talented, but then, with a mother like Serena, it was hardly surprising.

"Donna's going to play an accompaniment to one of the hymns and I believe Carmen will be singing."

"It's so exciting," sighed Asa, who'd finished washing Floria's hair and was wrapping it in a toweled turban. "I wonder if Stormzy is going to be there? He's so fit. Now that's someone I'd like to meet."

"I'm not sure Serena was into gangster rap," said Krish, flicking one of her braids.

Daisy laughed as Asa scowled at him.

Floria moved from the sink to a workstation, holding the turban in place. "I'm going to ask the girls to stay with me at Brompton Court after the service. It seems rude not to, especially because I've got eight bedrooms at my disposal."

"I think that's a fabulous idea," said Daisy. "Are they arriving today?"

She nodded. "Yes, but I think they already have accommodation for tonight. Besides, they'll be exhausted after their flights, especially Mimi, who's come all the way from Australia. Greg said he'd let them know they are welcome to stay at Brompton Court."

"Is your father staying there too?" asked Daisy. Floria's little flat in Mayfair was only a one-bedroom.

"Oh yes, he loves Brompton Court. He designed the rose garden, you know." She got a faraway look in her eyes. "I still remember how he planned it down to the last tiny detail, guided by his friend, Alan Titchmarsh, and then, once it was done, he spent every weekend there, pruning and attending to the roses. He knew all the varietals by name." She sighed wistfully. "It bought him endless joy. I think he missed his roses more than my mother when they split up. She was never one for gardening."

Daisy doubted Serena ever gave the garden a second thought, other than when she was seducing her latest lover behind the hedgerows. "If they agree to stay with you, it will give you all a wonderful chance to get to know one another."

Floria met her gaze in the mirror and her voice faltered. "I'm so nervous, Dais. What if they don't like me? They're all so talented and so musical. Not like me. I can't play an instrument to save my life, and my voice is nothing to write home about. How did Serena's genes skip me entirely?"

"Don't be silly, Flo. You're bubbly and vivacious, and you have an incredible way with people. Everybody loves you. You're the friendliest person I know." She gave her friend a hug. "Trust me, they're going to adore you."

Floria gave a tremulous smile. "I hope so. My stomach is in knots just thinking about it."

"It'll all be fine. I promise. Besides, I'll be there to hold your hand."

"Thanks, Daisy. You're the best." She took a shaky breath.

"What's not to love?" Krish gave her shoulder a quick

squeeze on his way to the front of the salon, where his next client was waiting. Floria smiled at him.

"Hello, Mrs. Roberts," he gushed as a smart, middle-aged woman in a two-piece suit stood up from the sofa. "Sorry to keep you waiting. Do come and take a seat at the basin."

Daisy smiled at Floria. "Now, do you want the usual, or shall I crop it a bit to make it more on trend?"

"Crop it," said Floria, never one to back down from a challenge. "I need to upgrade my look. I don't want to be the dowdy younger sister."

Daisy grinned. "You could never be that." With Floria's effervescent personality, pale golden curls and glittering blue eyes, she was always the center of attraction. She radiated positivity and good humor, which made people gravitate toward her. No, "dowdy" was not a word Daisy would ever associate with her friend.

Then she got to work.

"So, I heard that Tatiana and her boyfriend confessed to breaking into Brompton Court," said Floria when Daisy was almost finished with the cut. "DI McGuinness didn't seem to think they'd stolen the Modigliani, though, which I thought was rather odd, considering they admitted to being there."

This wasn't news to Daisy, who'd also spoken to McGuinness earlier that morning. After their conversation last night, they'd developed a mutually respectful relationship, and Daisy was flattered that the normally uncommunicative detective had thought to phone her to tell her the outcome of the interrogation. But then, she had been the one to tell him Sergio's alibi didn't check out.

"Apparently, Sergio let himself in using Tatiana's key

around two in the morning and found Serena lying on the floor. He panicked and took off. He claims he didn't enter the house." She relayed what DI McGuinness had told her.

"But do you believe him?" asked Floria.

"Serena was killed shortly after midnight, so if he really did go at two in the morning, he couldn't have killed Serena. Anyway, he doesn't strike me as the murdering type."

Liz Roberts, who was chairwoman of the Edgemead Women's Institute and a formidable figure in the community, looked out from under her silver-foil wraps. "I wouldn't trust him, Floria dear. Those criminal types will say anything to get off the hook. He could quite easily lie about the time he was there. In fact, he's probably got the painting stashed away somewhere right now, waiting for the heat to die down."

"A painting like that would be very hard to fence," pointed out Daisy, who knew a little about the art world.

Floria, who knew a lot more, agreed. "Absolutely, a Modigliani is so instantly recognizable, especially if it's been reported stolen, that no self-respecting art dealer would touch it. It could only be sold on the black market, and I doubt Sergio has those kinds of contacts."

"Collin might," mused Daisy, earning herself a startled look from her friend.

"I thought he'd been cleared?"

"He has," said Daisy. "I was just thinking out loud."

"Hmm . . . " Floria admired her new haircut in the mirror. "Great job, by the way. I love it."

"Thanks. It'll look even better when it's dried."

Floria turned around in the chair. "I don't know, Dais.

It seems like a hell of a coincidence that Mother was murdered the same night Sergio broke in to steal the Modigliani."

Daisy tapped the comb against her cheek. Floria did have a point, and normally she wouldn't go in for coincidences, but something about this one didn't make sense.

"Sergio insisted Serena was already dead when he got there. He said all he wanted was the painting. He's a petty criminal—he served time in Poland for theft—and when Tatiana told him Serena would be drunk and alone on Saturday night, he saw an opportunity."

"I knew he was dangerous," piped up Krish from across the room. "I could see it in his slanting, gypsy eyes."

"Who's to say he didn't kill her, then steal the painting?" interjected Liz, refusing to let it go.

Daisy flashed her an irritated look. "He's a small-time crook, an opportunist, not a cold-blooded murderer. It's a whole different psyche."

"I think you're taking your studies too literally," Floria said kindly as Daisy plugged in the hair dryer. "People don't always fit into neat psychological categories. With the right motivation, anyone can kill."

"I'd tend to agree with that," said Liz.

"Don't you need to rinse off that tint now, Mrs. Roberts?" asked Daisy, raising her eyebrows at Krish.

Once Krish had led her to the basin, Daisy said, "Do you really believe that, Flo?"

Floria swiveled around to face her. "Okay, most people. Wouldn't you if your child was threatened, or someone you loved was in danger?"

Daisy threw her hands in the air, still holding the hair

dryer. "Okay, you might have a point, but those are unusual circumstances. Sergio had nothing against Serena. He didn't even know her. This was just a burglary. Besides, his fingerprints weren't found anywhere inside the house."

"He could have worn gloves."

Daisy sighed. "That's true, but without any evidence they can't hold him."

"So my mother's killer is still out there?"

Daisy grimaced. "It looks that way."

The hair dryer was far too loud for sensible conversation, but the minute Daisy switched it off, Floria put down the *Cosmopolitan* magazine she'd been browsing and said, "Now tell me, Daisy, what's happening with this hunky Irish police detective? Has he made a move on you yet?"

Daisy was momentarily stunned. She had been miles away, her mind on the dwindling suspect list and looking for possibilities that may or may not be there.

She covered by pretending outrage. "Floria, I've only just met him, and no, he hasn't made a move on me." She shook her head. "Nor is he likely to. We're working together to solve this case, that's all. He values my input. Besides, you know I'm not interested in dating anyone."

"Hmm . . . I've seen the way he looks at you and I'm sure it's not just your input he values."

At Daisy's exasperated look, she grinned, "Anyway, it's been almost two years since Tim left. You have to move on. It's time, Daisy."

Daisy bit her lip. She wasn't so sure. Tim's abandonment had left her feeling raw and vulnerable, and she didn't think she would ever be ready to put herself in that position again.

"I think Paul McGuinness is just what you need to get over Tim," Floria insisted. "What do you think, Daisy? How about a nice, casual fling—nothing serious—just to get you out of the rut you're in."

"She's right, darling," Krish interjected as he led Liz, freshly washed, back to the mirror. "You really do need to get back in the game. You'll forget how to play at this rate."

"Can we change the topic, please?" All this talk of Paul was making her uncomfortable. "The man might be married for all we know."

"Oh, he's not." Krish waved the hair dryer at her. "I asked my friend Craig, whose sister works at Guildford Police Station, and she said he's single. All the girls secretly fancy him, but he shuts them down. No one can get close." He gave Daisy a knowing grin. "Perhaps you'll be the lucky lady to break through that hard, macho exterior."

"Okay, enough of this." Daisy put on her boss voice. "Back to work, everyone."

Floria laughed. "You're so predictable, Dais. By the way, you're more than welcome to stay at Brompton Court too. You know that, right?"

"Thanks, hun, but I'm so close it's hardly worth it." She hesitated, then asked, "Will you move back there permanently if you inherit the place?"

"I don't know," she admitted as Daisy rubbed some gel onto the ends of her freshly cropped curls. "My job is in the West End, so it'll be one hell of a commute, and I've got my little flat. I think I'll probably just come back on weekends. My father might move back now that Mother's gone. He is getting on a bit, so it'll be good to have him in the country, and Violeta and Pepe will be there to look after the place."

"Speaking of the Bonellos." Daisy admired her handiwork and kept her voice light. "Did you know about Pepe's condition?"

"No." Floria frowned in alarm. "What condition? Is he ill?"

"He's got rheumatoid arthritis in his hands. It's crippling him, apparently. Ruth from the doctor's office says he needs an operation, but the waiting times are astronomical."

Floria's eyes widened. "I had no idea. Poor Pepe. I wonder why Violeta didn't mention it."

"That's what I was thinking. She must have known you'd want to help."

"She probably didn't want to bother me with it, what with Mother's murder and all that."

Daisy gnawed on her lower lip. There was no easy way to say this. She decided to just come right out with it. "You don't think they would have tried to steal the Modigliani, do you? To pay for his medical bills?"

"No!" gasped Floria, jumping out of her chair. "I can't believe they'd resort to something like that. They're not criminals. They'd come to me, first, surely?"

Daisy said softly, "You said yourself, anyone could be capable under the right circumstances. What if they had no other way of financing the operation? What if they meant to steal the painting and not harm anyone, but then Serena caught them in the act?"

Floria shook her head so violently that Daisy put a steadying hand on her shoulder. "No, I'm sorry, Daisy, I won't believe it. I've known them most of my life and they wouldn't do something like this, not even if they were desperate."

"Okay, okay. I'm sorry, it was just a thought." She didn't want Floria getting too upset. The Bonellos were a sweet, elderly couple, after all, and Violeta had been so kind to Floria over the years. "I can't see them resorting to murder either. I just mentioned it because they are the only other people who have a key, and we know the locks weren't forced."

"You mean apart from me, all of Serena's ex-husbands, and the maid? Any one of our keys could have been stolen or copied. Or perhaps Mother let in her killer? It's quite possible she knew him or her." Daisy had to admit those were all possibilities. "You haven't lost your key, have you?"

"No, it's right here on my key fob. I'll ask Father if he's still got his, although I suspect he misplaced it years ago. He's a bit scatty like that."

Daisy raised her eyebrows. "The murderer could have got hold of it somehow. Please ask him as soon as you can, Floria."

"I will." She paused to look at her reflection.

"See, not dowdy in the slightest," joked Daisy.

Floria grinned, her natural exuberance returning. "If I do end up in *Hello!* magazine, at least I'll have great hair!"

"I'm sorry if I upset you," said Daisy, feeling guilty about shocking her friend. Floria was such a loving person, she couldn't see the bad in anybody. "But we have to consider all options, no matter how unlikely."

"I know." Floria sighed. "That's what I love about you,

Dais. You're so logical. I'd make a terrible detective. I'm always too willing to believe people."

"That's what I love about you." Daisy smiled. Then, as an afterthought, she added, "You know, DI McGuinness is going to be looking at all Serena's ex-husbands as potential suspects, so if we can establish where their keys are, that will be a good start."

Floria nodded. "I'm on it. Don't worry."

Krish chimed in, "Naughty Collin was shacked up with his mistress in Lourmarin and Niall was chasing horse-flesh in Argentina, so you can rule them out."

"We still need to know where their keys are," persisted Daisy.

Floria put her hands on her friend's shoulders. "I'll call and ask them tonight. Will that make you happy?"

Daisy broke into a bright smile. "You know it will."

Chapter Thirteen

The sun was a deep orange disc low in the sky when Daisy said goodbye to her last customer. The High Street basked in a soft, amber glow that radiated off the church spire like a shimmering sign from above. It had been a busy day, and with Krish having the afternoon off to go shopping for his boyfriend in central London, they'd all had to pull their weight. She and Penny had split Krish's customers between them, many of whom were disappointed he wasn't there as it meant they weren't able to catch up on all the latest gossip. For many of her older clients, the hair salon was their only social outing of the day. The neighborhood care bus collected them outside their sheltered and semisheltered apartments and drove them into the village to do a spot of shopping and get their hair done before taking them back home again. They loved Krish, who made them laugh with his outrageous stories.

Daisy set about cleaning up the salon. It was her evening ritual. She would turn up Classic FM, sweep the floors, wipe the surfaces and polish the mirrors before spraying jasmine- and lilac-scented air freshener around the room.

When the place was spotless, she'd go out the front, locking the door behind her, a feeling of pride in her chest. Asa was kept busy sweeping, making tea and coffee and being the general dogsbody throughout the day, so Daisy usually let her go after her last hair wash. It suited Daisy, because she valued the quiet time at the end of the day in which to unwind and compose her thoughts. It might sound strange, but she found the cleaning therapeutic. She was polishing a mirror, window cleaner in one hand, a paper towel in the other, when there was a knock on the door. Turning, she saw the broad silhouette of Paul McGuinness standing outside. His features were obscured, but the sun had turned the ends of his hair a pinkish copper, and with his strong profile and square outline, he looked like the hero in a Japanese anime cartoon.

Whipping off her rubber gloves, she rushed to let him in.

"Hi, Paul, come in. I've been thinking about you all day."

"You have?" There was a definite sparkle in his eyes.

"Oops, that didn't come out right." She flushed and turned away to hide it. "I meant, I've been thinking about the case all day. Did you manage to speak to Collin?"

He laughed and shrugged off his jacket, throwing it onto the arm of the sofa. "Yes, I interviewed Collin this morning, and he confirmed he was with his mistress, Bernadette. They met in Marseilles on Saturday night and spent the weekend, including Monday and Tuesday, together. He had no idea his wife had been murdered until the French authorities contacted him last night at the guesthouse."

Daisy turned down the radio to a sensible volume. "So he's in the clear, then?"

Paul sat on the sofa, stretching out his legs in front of him. With his six-foot-plus height and wide shoulders, he made it look absurdly small.

"It looks like it. Bernadette backed up his story, and the owner of the guesthouse confirmed they checked in on Saturday evening at eight twenty." He sighed. "There's no way he could have murdered Serena."

Daisy toyed with the idea of sitting down, but then perched on the arm of the sofa instead. There didn't seem to be much room next to him. "So, where does that leave us?"

His stormy gaze met hers. "With not much to go on, unfortunately. Did you manage to find out who still has keys to the house?"

She'd texted him earlier that day to say Floria was doing some digging. "All Serena's ex-husbands had keys at one point, and as far as I can tell, none of them returned them after their divorces. Silly, really, when you consider how many antiques and works of art there are in that mansion."

Paul shook his head. "You'd think someone with Serena Levanté's wealth would be more careful."

Daisy straightened her dress and hoped she didn't smell of detergent. "Serena wasn't like that. All she cared about was her music. Monetary things weren't important to her. The valuable paintings were mostly acquired by Collin, except Serena's portrait, which was a commission, and the Stubbs Sir Ranulph gave to Floria. The antique furniture was Hubert's doing; he's in the antiques business, has a little shop off Portobello Road. I don't think Serena ever decorated. Besides, those men were all part of her life at some point; she probably trusted them."

Because that's what women did.

She thought back to Tim, who'd torn her heart to shreds when he'd disappeared out of her life two years before with no warning.

Nothing.

Not even a parting glance.

One day she'd got back from work and he was gone. Just like that. Taking all his belongings with him.

But she didn't want to dwell on that now. She blew a strand of hair out of her face and looked at Paul. He was handsome in a rough, no-nonsense sort of way, with that strong jawline covered in stubble and his unusual gray eyes. His hair was messy, like he'd run his hand through it too many times and now it had given up trying to behave and stood on end of its own accord.

Daisy continued, "She wouldn't have expected any of them to rob her, let alone kill her."

"Still, we have to check."

Expect the unexpected. It was a good motto to live by.

"I asked Floria to look into it. As you know, Niall— Serena's second husband, the horse breeder—was in Argentina at the time of her murder. He's just got back and says he still has his key but hasn't used it since he lived there, which was over a decade ago."

"Are we sure it hasn't been used by anyone else?"

"He keeps it in his safe, and Floria made him check it was still there. I think we can scratch him off the list."

Paul rubbed his stubble, which made a scratchy noise that for some odd reason reminded her of living with a man, with Tim. It wasn't a sound you often heard living alone.

"Okay, what about the others?" asked Paul.

She flicked her hair out of her face. "Hubert—Serena's third husband, the antique dealer—lives in Notting Hill with his partner, Lucian." At Paul's raised eyebrow, she explained, "He was always gay, although not overtly so, but it's bizarre Serena didn't cotton on sooner. They were party buddies and he helped her through a rough patch, so I think she felt indebted to him, which in her muddled brain translated into love, but that's a mystery we'll probably never solve."

"His key?" Paul cut to the chase.

"He has it in his bureau drawer. He checked, and it was there. Again, it hadn't been used since he lived at Brompton Court."

"I hope your friend is going to get the locks changed," he muttered. "It's a nightmare, having all these spare keys around. Anyone could waltz in at any time and steal any number of things. I saw that Stubbs you mentioned and a nice little Pissarro at the house the other day and I'm guessing they aren't fakes?"

"You know your artists," remarked Daisy.

"You sound surprised."

"It's not every day you meet a cultured police detective who appreciates art and speaks French like a native."

He avoided her gaze. "What about Sir Ranulph?"

Daisy shrugged. "His is the only key we can't locate. As you know, he lives in the south of France, near Avignon, and has no idea what happened to the key. He thinks he may have left it at Brompton Court when he moved out, which was over fifteen years ago. He hasn't used it since. Every time he visits, he's let in by the housekeeper."

Paul frowned. "We'll have to search the house for the

missing key. It might be among Serena's things, or in a drawer with other keys, that sort of thing."

"Knowing Sir Ranulph, it could even be at his house in France, buried among boxes of music scores or something. We might never find it."

"It's worth a look, don't you think? If we do find it at Brompton Court, we can focus on other lines of inquiry. If we don't, well, that could be how the killer got in."

"And you don't think Serena let her killer in herself?"

He gnawed gently on his lower lip. Daisy found the gesture quite sensual and averted her eyes. "I can't see it," said Paul. "She was drunk, still in her outfit from earlier that day, and besides, she fell from the landing. Why would she let him in and go back upstairs to the bedroom, only to be pushed over the balustrade?"

"It could have been someone she was taking to bed with her."

Paul stared at her for a long moment until Daisy felt a smidgeon of heat steal into her cheeks. Then he pursed his lips. "In that state? At that hour? I supposed it's possible, but unlikely. Would you welcome a man into your bed after midnight when you'd been drinking all day? Without changing your clothes, or even washing your face or re-applying your makeup?"

Daisy gazed at Paul but didn't reply. If she liked someone enough, she might. Dutch courage and all that. But somehow, she didn't think that was the case here. Paul was right. Serena was in no fit state to welcome a male guest.

She took a deep breath. "Of course, we're assuming Serena's killer was a man."

Paul looked pensive. "I am keeping an open mind on that score, but the probability is that it's a man."

There was a small pause, then Daisy said, "How do you propose we find this missing key?"

"I can send in a team to search the place."

"Oh no," said Daisy hastily, horrified at the thought of a search team messing up the house before Floria was inundated with guests. "Why don't you let me and Floria handle it? The memorial is on Friday, and I know Floria's got the cleaners in today and tomorrow."

"Cleaners will complicate matters," Paul remarked, the irritation evident in his tone. "They shift things around, destroy evidence."

"I know, but Floria has to get the place ready for her guests." As cultured as he was, he wouldn't understand the intricacies of managing an eight-bedroom mansion. To be fair, not many people would. The only reason Daisy knew what was involved was because she'd been friends with Floria for a long time, and she'd helped prepare for countless garden parties, soirées and impromptu concerts. Close friends and international guests expected to stay over, and the bedrooms had to be immaculate. That meant beds made up with fresh linen, pillows plumped, towels put out and fireplaces cleaned.

Eight times over.

Then, there was the food to order, not only for the reception, but to feed the guests who were staying on the property. Caterers were providing the eats after the memorial service, but Violeta had to order in extra essentials like bread, milk and eggs for breakfast and stock up on tea and coffee and little nibbles, should any of the guests get hungry. Including her half sisters and Sir Ranulph, Floria would have a full house. Lord and Lady Balfour expected a room because they were old friends of Serena and Sir Ranulph, who now lived in Monaco. Colonel Snodgrass was always allocated a room at Serena's parties because he was too old and doddery to get home by himself, particularly after a bottle of Collin's fine brandy. The final houseguest was a dazzling mezzo-soprano from America who Serena used to know but, according to Floria, was always more of a rival than a friend. Brompton Court would be packed to capacity.

A gardening service had to be bought in to help Pepe mow the extensive lawns, clean the fish pond and trim the herbaceous borders. It was a mammoth project, and one Floria usually handled with aplomb; however, having a police search team on the premises would throw her right off.

"We'll make sure we do a thorough search, including Serena's bedroom and office, which is where the key is most likely to be, if it's in the house at all."

He grunted. "I suppose that'll have to do. Let me know when you're there. I'd like to join you. Forensics have processed the study, the hall and the staircase, and we've done a general search of the premises, but we weren't looking for a missing key at that point."

"Okay, sure, and speaking of guests, did you manage to track down any of the sisters today?"

He looked smug. "I did indeed."

Daisy pursed her lips. "Do tell."

"Mimi arrived first thing this morning. I met her at Heathrow. I thought I'd combine British hospitality with a quick, informal interview."

Daisy was impressed. He didn't miss a beat.

"She was very tired and didn't say much, but I got the feeling she was overwhelmed by the course of events. She hadn't known she was adopted, a fact she was quite upset about. I will have to question her again more fully once she's acclimatized."

"What was she like?" asked Daisy, wondering whether the other sisters were anything like Floria.

"Angry." He gave a little shrug. "One of those rebellious types, I think. She has short hair with silver streaks in it and an eyebrow ring, if that helps."

Daisy was surprised. "Not at all like Floria, then?"

He shook his head. "No. I couldn't see any obvious similarities. She's shorter, dark-haired with an olive complexion, not an English rose like Floria. They couldn't be more different, in fact."

"That's interesting," mused Daisy. "What about Donna?"

"I saw her this afternoon. She's staying in Esher at a local bed-and-breakfast. She's lovely-looking but very reserved, didn't offer up much in the way of useful information. Her parents had told her she was adopted, but they didn't know Serena Levanté was her birth mother. Apparently, it said something different on the birth certificate."

"So, Serena changed her name," said Daisy. "I suppose it's not that unusual. A lot of celebrities do it."

"She seems nice, albeit a bit quiet, and her eyes were red, like she'd been crying."

"Did you ask her what was wrong?" Daisy wanted to know.

He shrugged. "I asked her if anything was the matter, but she said she was fine, and I didn't want to push."

"And you call yourself a detective," Daisy tutted.

"My skills lie more on the interrogation side," he said, a grim expression on his face. "I'm not very good at coercing information out of distraught females."

"Thank goodness you have me," breathed Daisy.

At that moment Paul's stomach rumbled. He stood up. "I'd better get something to eat before I head home. Can you recommend a restaurant or takeaway close by? Something cheap and cheerful?"

Daisy smiled. "I can do one better. I'll show you. Just let me grab my jacket."

She'd have to come in early tomorrow morning to straighten up. The cleaning materials were still lying on the coffee table, along with her rubber gloves and wads of used paper towels. "There's a small Italian place around the corner that does amazing pizza and pasta, and a passable pinot grigio."

"Sounds perfect."

As they strolled down the street, Daisy asked about Carmen. It was getting dark and the streetlights had already been switched on. She loved the old-fashioned design of the lampposts, unchanged since Victorian times. She often pictured the lamplighters on their ladders, lighting the wicks at dusk and extinguishing them at dawn. This being a quintessential English village, most of the shops had closed for the day so the High Street was quiet, with only a handful of people still scattered about.

Paul gave an exaggerated sigh. "She's a tough nut to crack. I went to her room at the Hilton in Park Lane, but she wasn't in. Her phone went straight to voice mail. If she's in the country, she doesn't want to be contacted."

"The Hilton in Park Lane." Daisy raised an eyebrow.

"I believe it's in her boyfriend's name. He's some hotshot fashion photographer."

"Interesting, I wonder if he'll be at the memorial service too?"

Paul shrugged. "I've no idea, but I'll have to question her at some point. She can't avoid me forever."

"It's up here," said Daisy as they turned a corner and walked up a small side street. Up ahead, a red awning could be seen hanging over an illuminated window complete with flowering window boxes and hanging strands of garlic. The sign above the door read "Nonna Lina." Inside looked warm and inviting.

"Very quaint," he commented, opening the door and standing back so Daisy could enter.

"*Buona sera*, Cristiano," sang Daisy once they were inside. A middle-aged man with a mop of dark hair graying at the temples came out to greet them. He kissed Daisy on both cheeks. "*Mia caro*, how are you?"

"I'm well, thanks. How is Greta?"

His hands traced the shape of a big ball in front of his stomach. "She's about to pop, I think."

Daisy laughed, then turned to Paul, who was waiting patiently behind her. "This is my friend, Paul." She purposely left off his title; he probably didn't want to be seen as an officer of the law when he went out for a casual bite to eat. "Greta, Cristiano's wife, is pregnant with their fifth child."

Impressed, Paul shook his hand. "Congratulations."

Cristiano beamed. "Ah, *Commissario*. You are the policeman working on the murder of Señora Levanté? I heard all about you." He came in closer. Paul could smell the smoke from the pizza oven on his clothing. "Tell me, do you know who killed her?"

So much for that. It seemed the mystery of Serena's murder had gripped the entire community. He shot Daisy an awkward grin. "That's right. Pleased to meet you, and no, not yet, but we're working on it."

"Such a voice!" He kissed his fingertips. "My mama says not even Cecilia Bartoli can sing like that."

Daisy raised an eyebrow. "That's quite a compliment coming from Mama Lina."

Cristiano nodded seriously. Then he gestured to a table. "Please, sit down and I will bring you some wine. You like the usual?"

Paul tried but failed to hide a smirk.

"I come here a lot," Daisy muttered, sitting down at a table for two next to a wall covered in a massive, hand-painted mural of Napoli. Mount Vesuvius stood majestically in the background behind the town, while the Bay of Naples glistened invitingly in the foreground.

"Evidently." He sat, turning his body at an angle so his long legs wouldn't touch hers under the table.

They ordered the specialty pizza, which consisted of salami, avocado, cherry tomatoes and a sprinkling of sesame seeds, and drank the house wine while they waited. She noticed Paul only had half a glass, which he sipped slowly.

"So, where did you learn to speak French so well?" Daisy asked. It seemed a safe topic to start off the conversation.

"My mother was French," he said nonchalantly. "We spoke it a lot at home."

"That explains it. I knew it was more than school French. I studied it up to GCSE level and I can't speak it nearly as fluently as you."

He shifted in his chair and glanced around the restaurant, as if admiring the decor.

Daisy studied him over her glass. He seemed defensive

all of a sudden, and she got the impression he didn't like talking about his personal life.

Who *did?* she thought grimly.

Not wanting to make him uncomfortable, she changed the subject and brought the conversation round to the investigation. "Did Collin say why he lied about where he was going? Violeta thought he was in the Bahamas."

"Yeah, he admitted he didn't want Serena to know where he was in case she tried to go after him, so he said he was going to the Bahamas, thinking it would be too far away for her to follow him."

"Hmm . . . plausible, I suppose." There was a pause, and then she said, "I'm thinking out loud here, but is it possible the Modigliani was stolen prior to the murder? I'm not sure Serena would have even noticed if it had gone because she doesn't go into Collin's study. He keeps it locked."

Paul's eyes narrowed. "Are you implying the painting could have been stolen earlier that day, or perhaps even days before we noticed it was gone?"

"It's just a thought . . . " Then she shook her head. "Actually, no. Scrap that. Violeta would have noticed if it wasn't there."

"If she went into the study."

"I'll ask her, shall I?" Daisy dug in her handbag for her phone. At that minute the pizzas arrived. They smelled fantastic. Cristiano smiled gleefully and told them to enjoy before rushing back to the kitchen. The taverna was filling up now with a constant stream of patrons filing in through the door.

"Yes, ask her," said Paul, before grabbing a slice and

taking an enormous bite. "This is seriously good." He popped the rest of the slice into his mouth.

Daisy put her phone on the table and took a slice herself. She was starving too, and no one made pizza quite like Cristiano and his brother, Guido, who was the chef. After a couple of slices to satisfy her hunger, she wiped her hands on a napkin, had a sip of wine and picked up her phone.

At that same moment, the surface lit up and it began to ring.

"Typical," she muttered, glancing at Paul. "It's Floria. I'd better get this."

She answered, then listened intently, her brow twisting into a frown.

"He's here," she said, her voice low. "I'll let him know."

"What's wrong?" Paul put the slice he was about to eat back down on the plate. "Has something happened?"

Daisy blinked at him, a cascade of thoughts tumbling through her mind.

How? Why?

It didn't make sense.

Paul leaned forward, his eyes wide. "Daisy? What is it?"

She stared back at him.

"The Modigliani's been found."

Chapter Fourteen

It was a cold, dark night with no moon to speak of, and their previous lighthearted mood seemed to have dissipated, along with the warmth of the day. Paul drove them up the winding drive toward Brompton Court, his black BMW handling the curves with ease. Although the house was lit up, the woods at the bottom of the garden looked sinister and impenetrable. Daisy suppressed a shudder. "I don't have a good feeling about this," she murmured.

Floria let them in, her face flushed from the discovery. "Oh, Daisy. Violeta is in a state. She found the Modigliani in the priest hole under the pantry. Who could have put it there?"

"Someone who knew the house intimately," growled DI McGuinness. "May I see it?"

"Of course."

Floria led them through the entrance hall where Serena had died to the large, rustic kitchen with its wooden ceiling beams and terra-cotta-tiled floor. Violeta sat hunched at the kitchen table, shaking her head.

"I don't understand," she kept repeating.

Floria put an arm around her. "Violeta is in considerable shock."

Paul stood beside the table. "Where is the painting now?"

"It's still in there," said Floria, nodding toward the pantry. "We haven't touched anything in case you wanted to dust for fingerprints."

Paul gave a small grunt of approval. "There's a forensic technician on the way. Can I see the hiding place?"

Floria showed him into a spacious pantry filled with well-stocked shelves containing everything from baking ingredients to cured ham and bottles of pickles and caviar. The light was bright because there were no windows and the walls were made of thick stone, which meant it was considerably colder in this room than anywhere else in the house. She bent down and pointed beneath the bottom shelf, which was at knee level. Paul crouched down and saw a gaping hole about a meter wide by half a meter tall. It wasn't visible from a standing position, the bottom shelf effectively hiding it from view.

"That's the priest hole," she explained. "It's always kept shut and we only use it to store backup supplies like flour and sugar. Violeta was about to bake several cakes for the reception, so she opened it, and that's when she discovered the Modigliani."

Peering into the black hole, Paul could just about make out the glimmer of a gilded frame. The painting itself was in darkness; however, when Floria stood up, a shaft of light fell on the canvas and illuminated an angelic, oval face that stared up at him through the darkness. He wobbled in surprise. Daisy, who was peering over his shoulder, whispered, "She's beautiful."

Paul stood up, his knees complaining with a loud click. "We'd better wait for forensics."

"It's eerie seeing her lying there in the dark, isn't it?" Floria shivered. "Almost like she's begging to be rescued."

Paul didn't comment. He stalked out of the pantry and back into the nice, warm kitchen.

"How about some coffee?"

"I'll make it," said Daisy, glad for something to do.

Paul sat down at the table opposite Violeta, who seemed to have recovered a bit. Floria was holding her hand.

"Can you talk me through what happened?" he asked the housekeeper.

She looked up. "I wanted to make a panettone for tomorrow when the girls arrive. It was Serena's favorite, you know. I'd run out of flour, so I opened the compartment to get some more. That's when I saw it. Gave me quite the fright, staring back at me like that. I thought I'd seen a ghost."

The pale face on the painting did look extremely ghost-like, staring out of the gloom. Paul could sympathize. It would have given him a fright too.

"And you didn't touch it?"

Violeta shook her head. "No. It took me a minute to figure out what it was, then I called Floria."

"I was upstairs settling Father into one of the guest rooms," Floria explained. "We've had the cleaners here all day, so the place is livable again." She flashed Daisy a smile. "My sisters arrive tomorrow, so I wanted to get the house shipshape."

Daisy put down four steaming cups of coffee on the table, along with the milk carton and a sugar bowl. "Are you staying here as well?" Paul directed his question to Floria.

"Yes, it's easier to organize everything from here, and I've taken two weeks' compassionate leave from work. I'm in my old room in the east wing; that's where most of the guest rooms are. The west wing has been converted into Mother's suite, which is actually three rooms if you count her dressing room and office, and then there's Collin's study."

Paul raised an eyebrow. "Not short of space, are you?"

Floria smiled indulgently. "You'd be surprised. We'll have a full house this weekend."

Daisy poured a little milk into her coffee. She noticed Paul drank his dark and strong. No milk or sugar. It suited his personality.

Floria turned to him and asked, "Did you meet my sisters today? I know Daisy said you were going to try to interview them."

Paul nodded. "I met two of them, yes."

"And?" Floria gazed at him hopefully. It was clear she was desperate for information.

"Mimi was tired from the flight, so I didn't speak to her for very long. I just gave her a lift to her hotel. She seems very nice."

"And Donna?"

"She was fairly reserved, although she also seemed very nice."

Daisy sighed. *Nice?* That was all he had to say?

Paul really wasn't very good at this.

"Mimi is short, with dark hair and an eyebrow ring," she cut in, giving Paul an exasperated look. "While Donna is beautiful, but a bit quiet. Those were your first impressions, weren't they?"

Paul seemed happy for Daisy to elaborate, so she continued. "And neither knew Serena was their birth mother. They were both still in shock at hearing the news."

"What about Carmen?" Floria wanted to know.

Paul shrugged. "Couldn't get hold of her. She seems to be off-the-grid right now, but we'll track her down at the funeral tomorrow."

They discussed the Modigliani for a while, then Paul put down his empty coffee cup. "While we're here, we may as well have a quick look for that key."

"What key? You mean Father's lost key?" asked Floria.

"Yes, you mentioned he might have left it here at some point," said Daisy. "Do you know where Serena would keep any spare house keys?"

"In the hall cabinet," said Violeta immediately. "There's a drawer containing all the spare keys."

"I'll have a look." Floria got up and left the kitchen, Daisy right behind her.

They rummaged through the drawer, but apart from Serena's set, which had a diamanté pendant on it in the shape of a music note, they didn't find any others.

"It doesn't look like it's here." Floria blew a strand of hair off her forehead. "Could it be anywhere else, Violeta?"

"No, I don't think so. I put all the keys I find in here."

"What about Serena's bedroom or office?" asked Daisy.

Violeta shook her head. "She always leaves her drawers open, so I put her things away and close them again. There are no keys in there; I'm sure of it. But of course, you are welcome to look yourself."

"Perhaps I'll go up and have a quick peek," said Floria, who knew Daisy would be itching to do so. "I'll be right back."

She left the others at the foot of the stairs. Not five minutes later she was back. "Violeta is right. There's not a single key in any of Mother's drawers in her bedroom or study. Maybe Father was mistaken and it is at his house in France?"

Daisy sighed. "I don't know, but it would help to find it. That way we can rule out someone stealing it to gain entry."

"I doubt we'll ever find it," said Floria, crestfallen. "I'm going to have to change the locks, aren't I?"

"It would be a good idea," said Paul. "In fact, I'd get it done as soon as possible."

Everyone was thinking the same thing. There was a killer on the loose who may have a key to Brompton Court.

"Hmm . . . I'll call the locksmith first thing tomorrow morning."

At that moment, a key turned in the lock and the front door opened, making them jump.

"Is it true? Has it been found?" Collin blustered in, looking disheveled, his hair windswept and the buttons on his jacket done up incorrectly.

Paul stepped forward. "Mr. Harrison, please calm down. Yes, it's true. We've located your painting."

"Where the hell did you find it?" he bellowed. "Who stole it? Is it damaged? Because if it's damaged in any way, I swear I'll sue."

"We don't know that yet, but it was found on the premises."

"What? Here, at Brompton Court?" His voice dropped several decibels. "So it never left the property?"

"No, it seems that whoever stole it, hid it in the priest hole under the pantry," said Floria, earning herself a stern look from DI McGuinness. "Oops, sorry, wasn't I supposed to say anything?"

"I think he'd have preferred to keep the location a secret," whispered Daisy.

"It doesn't matter now," said Paul gruffly. "Mr. Harrison, we've got forensics on the way, so I'm afraid you can't see the painting yet. Once we've analyzed it, you can have it back, but right now it's going to have to go into evidence while we process it."

"Can I at least see her?" He wrung his hands. "I've been so worried."

DI McGuinness sighed. "Okay, you can have a quick peek, but that's all." He escorted Collin to the pantry, leaving Daisy and Floria in the entrance hall.

The doorbell rang, loud and clear.

Floria, who was standing directly beneath it, nearly jumped out of her skin. "I swear, my shattered nerves."

It was only the forensic technician, a slim but good-looking lad wearing fashionable, black-rimmed spectacles and dressed in protective overalls, complete with gloves and booties. He carried an enormous metallic case containing his forensic equipment.

"I'm here for the painting," he gushed, his cheeks flushed with excitement.

"Floria, what on earth is going on down there?" came a frail voice from upstairs. Daisy looked up to see Sir Ranulph in his pajamas, standing on the landing. He was clutching the banister like he was afraid to fall over.

"It's okay, Dad. Nothing to worry about. I'll be up in a jiffy."

She glanced at Daisy. "I'd better go and tell him

what's happening. He doesn't even know we've found the Modigliani yet."

"I'll show him to the pantry."

Daisy beckoned to the technician to follow her. He beamed, picked up his case, and followed her like an eager puppy. If he had a tail, it would be wagging profusely.

"It is really a Modigliani?" he asked in a reverent tone, as if he couldn't quite believe his luck.

She smiled at his enthusiasm. "That it is."

Collin was in raptures at the discovery and had to be frog-marched out of the kitchen by a stony-faced DI McGuinness, who wanted nothing more than to get rid of him before he contaminated the scene. "Let's let the foren-sic technician do his work," he said firmly as he pushed him in the direction of the stairs. "I'll call you to let you know when you can have it back."

"I'm going to have a drink," Collin said defiantly. "This is still my house." And he marched off in the direction of the library.

Paul joined Violeta and Daisy in the kitchen while the gloved technician carefully removed the painting from its hiding place and wrapped it in cling film to keep any potential fingerprints intact.

"Righto, I'm going to put this in the van," he said, carrying it past them to the front door. A fine layer of white flour covered his overalls. The painting was still in its frame and looked to be undamaged, although the plastic wrapping obscured the detail.

"I'll give you a hand. It's time I got going too." Paul fetched the forensic kit from the pantry.

"Cheers, mate." The technician threw him a grateful grin.

Daisy and Floria walked with them to the front door.

"Thanks for stopping by, Inspector," said Floria, shooting a quick glance at Daisy. "I hope I didn't mess up your evening too much."

Paul grunted. "It's my job, Miss Levanté." He hesitated, then said, "Do you mind if I stop by tomorrow after the memorial service to have a word with your sisters? It shouldn't take too long."

"Of course. Do whatever you need to." Floria retreated to the kitchen, leaving Daisy to see DI McGuinness out.

"We'll have to take a rain check on the pizza," he said softly, hovering on the doorstep.

She smiled. "Maybe once you've solved this case."

He gave a curt nod, switching back to his business-like self. "Then let's hope we find some prints on that painting."

"Fingers crossed," she called as he strode to his car and climbed in, but at the back of her mind she was thinking that that would be far too easy.

Chapter Fifteen

Daisy watched the limousine pull up outside Brompton Court. It was a lovely, bright summer's day without a cloud in the sky, and the limousine, polished to a high shine, glistened like a sleek, black stallion.

"Floria!" she yelled for the third time. Her friend had tried on all the clothes in her closet and still couldn't settle on something to wear. Eventually, Daisy had given up and left her to it, preferring to wait downstairs in the parlor with Sir Ranulph.

"She's so good at organizing everyone else, but no good at organizing herself," said Sir Ranulph with a little shake of his head. "Three hundred people at a garden party doesn't faze her, but this memorial has quite undone her."

"I expect it's because she's about to meet her sisters," said Daisy, wondering how on earth he could have forgotten that fact. Floria's indecision wasn't so much about what to wear as the impression she wanted to give her sisters. She was so nervous to meet them that nothing she put on would be good enough.

"Ah, yes. The prodigal daughters return." He looked

toward the portrait of Serena hanging over the stairs. "I suppose it's as it should be."

Daisy frowned. The limo driver hooted the horn.

"Floria!" she yelled again.

Thankfully, Floria appeared on the landing in a black Hobbs dress with a matching blazer. On her head was an elegant fascinator made with black feathers and beading.

"I look awful," she said, her face flushed from pulling on and off various outfits. "Black is so unforgiving, and I've put on ten pounds since I last wore this, but it's the most appropriate thing in my wardrobe."

"Well, it's too late to change now," said Daisy, marching up the stairs to the landing. She took her friend's hand and led her down the stairs. "We have to go. The limousine is waiting."

"You look lovely, dear," said her father. "I don't know what all the fuss is about. No one's going to be looking at you when your mother's illegitimate offspring are making their debut. Stephen Springer from *The Star* has been phoning me all morning for an exclusive. He goes to my club."

"What did you tell him?" asked Floria, appalled. "We can't have the press at the reception; the girls will be overwhelmed enough as it is."

"I told him to bugger off, and he knows me well enough not to argue."

Daisy smiled. Sir Ranulph wasn't one to be pushed around. It was one of the reasons why he'd been such a successful music producer in his day. He'd managed Serena for over a decade, orchestrating her rise to fame, a feat many others had subsequently tried but failed to emulate.

Floria was very quiet as they drove to the church.

"Relax." Daisy squeezed her hand. "They're going to love you. It's all going to be fine, you'll see."

She got a tremulous smile in response. "I don't think I've ever been this nervous."

"The traffic is dire," said the driver, slowing to a crawl. "The road to the church is completely blocked."

"I knew this would happen," said Floria. "That's why I went in earlier this morning. The church looks incredible, by the way. The florist really outdid herself with the arrangements."

"You always make sure everything looks amazing," she said loyally. Floria really did have a gift for this kind of thing.

They crawled along for a few minutes before coming to a complete standstill. Daisy pushed the button to wind down the window. The approach road was bumper to bumper with taxis, BMWs, Mercedes-Benzes, Bentleys and Jaguars. All Serena's famous friends had turned out to say farewell, including the ones who were coming to ogle her illegitimate daughters, all of whom, it was understood, would inherit large fortunes. There was much speculation about Dame Serena's wealth, some saying she'd squandered her millions, others saying she was still worth a fortune, but Greg, Serena's solicitor, had been annoyingly tight-lipped about it, which didn't do anything to assuage the rumors.

Sir Ranulph leaned back and opened *The Times*. "There's no rush, Harry. It's not like they're going to start without us."

Daisy supposed that was one way of looking at it.

Eventually, they got there, and Harry opened the door for Sir Ranulph.

"Christ, what a crowd," he said, looking out, and for a moment Daisy thought he might duck back inside the car and ask to be taken home.

Floria took his arm. "Come on, Dad. We have to set a good example."

He didn't reply, but let his daughter lead him up the cobblestoned path to the church. The freshly mowed lawns on either side were packed with a dark sea of bodies, all dressed in somber funeral attire.

"I've never seen such an enormous turnout for a funeral," a gruff voice murmured in her ear. DI McGuinness stood beside her, smartly dressed in a black suit complete with silver cuff links. His sergeant wasn't with him. Daisy surveyed the crowd. There were easily several hundred people there, most of whom didn't have invitations to the church service, but who would listen outside, thanks to Floria's stroke of genius in installing loudspeakers.

"It's a memorial service, not a funeral. You need a body for that." It had been an annoyance on Floria's side that the medical examiner had refused to release the body until more tests had been done.

"Touché." He gave a little nod. "The ME says next week." Then the family would have a private burial, far from the prying eyes of the rest of the world.

Daisy said wistfully, "Dame Serena Levanté had millions of fans. Floria wanted anyone who knew and loved her to be able to pay their respects."

"And catch a glimpse of the illegitimate daughters," added Paul sardonically. They both knew he was right. That was primarily why the press was here. They knew a human-interest story when they saw one, and Dame Serena's three secret daughters welcomed back into the family fold after her mysterious death fit the billing to perfection.

"Did you manage to track down Carmen?" Daisy asked as she watched the vicar come outside and greet Sir Ranulph.

He shook his head. "Nope, but I can confirm she is here. I didn't think it was appropriate to question her before her mother's *memorial service*." He glanced at Daisy. "But I will corner her afterward at Brompton Court. I believe you're all going back there for lunch, before the reception?"

"Yes. Floria thought it would be a good idea for all the family to get together before the guests arrive."

"You're not family," he said slyly.

Daisy sniffed. "Close enough."

"Shall we?" Paul nodded toward the vicar who, flamboyant in purple robes, beckoned them in. The service was about to begin. Paul took a seat in the back pew, where his sergeant was waiting, fanning himself with the program. "I can shift over," he offered, but Daisy shook her head.

"I've got a seat reserved at the front."

He tilted his head. "See you later, then."

Daisy slipped into the second pew, behind the one reserved for the family. She had to admit the church looked beautiful. Pale flowers and candles adorned the altar, with little bunches on the end of every pew. Serena's *Best of* album played softly on repeat, serenading the guests as they filed in and took their places. Those without invitations to the service stood outside in the churchyard, listening over the loudspeakers. The press had set up camp across the road.

Daisy studied the Levanté sisters. From her position in the pew behind, she could only make out their profiles. Clutching a violin and looking extremely elegant in a black shift dress with a satin overlay was Donna. She held her head high, but nibbled her lower lip, a sign she was anxious. Next to her, sporting a defiant expression, was Mimi. The wild hair shot through with silver gave it away. Her shoulders were rigid and she jutted out her jaw as if to say, *Stare all you want; I don't care.* Then there was Carmen, who'd refused to sit in the family pew. The vicar, acting on Floria's instructions, approached her to ask if she wanted to join them, but she shook her head.

Not interested.

Daisy couldn't see her face, but her shoulders were stiff and unmoving, and like the others, she held her head high and stared straight in front of her, refusing to look at anyone. A hat with a delicate lace veil covered most of her face; only her chin and part of her cheek was visible.

Eventually, when the congregation was seated, the vicar began the proceedings. He waxed lyrical about Serena for a full five minutes before launching into a short sermon on how death wasn't the end—which nobody believed— before calling for the soloist. The congregation watched in breathless anticipation as Carmen rose out of her seat and made her way to the front of the church. So this was Serena's eldest, the opera singer who, if rumors were to be believed, had a voice to equal that of her mother.

Daisy heard a stricken Sir Ranulph whisper, "Oh, Lord. It's her."

It was true: Carmen was the splitting image of Serena, only younger and, if possible, more beautiful. Her dark hair hung in a silken shroud down her back, and now that she'd removed her hat with the lace veil, her olive skin and exquisite bone structure was revealed.

She turned and stared at the congregation through Serena's slanting, green cat eyes, heavily kohled, with a curious mixture of hostility and mirth. Daisy wondered why she was so antagonistic toward the rest of the family. Was her hatred of her biological mother so great that she couldn't bring herself to associate with her half sisters? And if so, that would give her the perfect motive for murder. The neglected eldest child . . . denied her birth right . . . would inherit on Serena's death. She made a mental note to talk to Paul about checking Carmen's flight details, although she was pretty sure he already had.

Carmen took a deep breath, composed herself and began to sing. "Amazing Grace" had never sounded more passionate or more heartfelt, and Daisy was certain she wasn't the only one whose skin prickled with goose bumps. Carmen held the audience captivated as her clear, iridescent soprano echoed through the church and out onto the village green, where members of the public listened in stunned silence. When she finished, there was a moment's pause before the congregation broke into thunderous applause. Outside, the clapping and cheering continued for a full five minutes.

And so a star is born, Daisy thought, meeting Floria's gaze and knowing she was thinking the same thing. With all the classical music producers, managers and other bigwigs in the congregation, Daisy was sure Carmen would be inundated by offers before she left the church.

The vicar could hardly speak, he was in such raptures. After a reading from Collin, he called on Floria to deliver the eulogy. Daisy felt sorry for her friend. Floria's relationship with Serena had been difficult, to say the least, and she knew how hard it had been for her to come up with flattering things to say about her mother. In the end, she'd settled for comments by friends and family, and those who had respected and revered Serena.

The remaining hymns were sung with rare gusto, no doubt inspired by Carmen's exquisite performance, and Donna, violin positioned neatly under her chin, accompanied them. As her slender fingers gripped the bow, her body moved with a fluid, forceful motion that was quite mesmerizing. Another musical talent, thought Daisy, impressed. She noticed Greg never once took his eyes off her. The solicitor was clearly smitten.

Then it was over. The guests trickled out of the church, Floria making a beeline for Carmen. "Come on. I've got to advise her not to commit to anyone before she gets besieged," she whispered as they fought their way through the crowd.

As expected, Carmen was surrounded by music industry professionals, all vying for her attention and shoving their cards under her nose. Daisy watched as Floria swept in and calmly took charge. This was pretty much what she did for a living, so she knew how to handle the scouts. Carmen, who had the terrified look of a deer in the headlights, sighed in relief as Floria fielded questions and offers, but accepted all business cards and let everyone know Carmen would call them back in due course.

"Nicely done," said Daisy as Floria led a bewildered Carmen down the path toward the waiting limo. Harry, the driver, had already shepherded Mimi and Donna into the air-conditioned vehicle where they waited for the others to join them.

"Thank you," breathed Carmen, still clutching her program. Daisy noticed her hands were shaking. "I never expected that."

Floria smiled. "It's an indication of how talented they think you are."

Carmen sniffed, her shoulders stiffening perceptibly. "Or because I'm *her* daughter." She couldn't even bring herself to say Serena's name.

Floria, who didn't have an aggressive bone in her body, turned Carmen around to face her. "Listen, they wouldn't approach you if you didn't have potential no matter whose daughter you were. And if you want my advice, pull every string you can, because this is a tough business and if you want to make it, you're going to need all the help you can get."

Carmen stared at her, then shrugged. "I'll bear that in mind."

"You should. It's what she does," Daisy said softly.

Carmen's eyes narrowed. The wall was back up.

"Excuse me," said a soft voice behind them. They all turned in annoyance at another interruption. A lanky, young man held up his hands in a gesture of apology. "I'm sorry to disturb you and I'm sure you've already been inundated with offers, but I'd like to represent you. My name is Jet Anderson. I work for Allegro Consulting."

"Allegro?" Floria, who was bustling Carmen into the limousine, paused. Daisy recognized the name. They were an up-and-coming music management company whose impressive portfolio was growing by the day.

He held out a card to Carmen. "Please, call me. I'd love to speak with you." He had mahogany eyes and dark, wayward hair, but his most striking feature was his height.

He was easily two inches taller than Carmen, who had Serena's commanding six-foot height and was wearing stilettos.

Carmen took the card and flashed him a rare smile. In fact, Daisy hadn't seen anything other than haughty contempt on her face since she'd arrived. Even Floria raised an eyebrow, but nodded her consent. "Come on, we've got to go. The press are coming."

Carmen ducked into the limousine.

"Just a minute, Miss Levanté, if I may . . . ?" An elderly man hurried down the path toward them. Floria turned, closing the car door behind her so her sisters were out of sight. Daisy helped Sir Ranulph, who'd been chatting to the vicar, into the vehicle from the other side. Out of the corner of her eye she watched Jet Anderson move away, a confident smile on his face.

"I wonder if I might have a minute?" The white-haired man took a moment to catch his breath. He had a heavy, German accent.

Floria waited rather impatiently. "How can I help you, sir?"

"I very much wanted to meet your sisters," he said, leaning down to peer in through the car window. Floria frowned and adjusted her position so she was blocking his view. She was about to say that it wasn't possible right now, but then he continued, "I delivered them, you see, in Vienna, thirty-two years ago."

Daisy and Floria both stared at him. That was the last thing they'd expected. DI McGuinness, who'd just joined them and overheard what the gentleman had said, was the first to find his tongue. "What is your name, sir?" he asked.

"Dr. Kurt Bachmann. I'm a retired gynecologist. I worked at Saint Anna Hospital in Vienna when Serena Levanté gave birth to her twins. I remember the day quite clearly."

Daisy met Paul's gaze. If this was true, the doctor could provide some very useful background information on Serena's past.

A crowd of reporters had gathered around the limousine and were pressing camera lenses to the windows. Harry revved the vehicle impatiently, no doubt spurred on by Sir Ranulph. Floria made a snap decision. "I'm sorry, Dr. Bachmann. As you can see, we really have to go now, but if you'd like to join us at the reception at Brompton Court, we can talk some more there. How does three o'clock sound?"

Daisy smiled gratefully at her friend.

"I'd be delighted," stammered the old man, visibly moved. "I've followed Serena's career most of my life. I'm a big fan of hers."

"Can I give you a lift somewhere?" offered Paul, nodding across the road. "My car is over there and my sergeant is waiting."

Daisy watched them walk off, the big detective next to the frail old man. Then she and Floria climbed into the limousine and out of the glare of the cameras. Things were definitely getting more interesting and they hadn't even had the reading of the will yet. The afternoon promised to be very revealing indeed.

Chapter Sixteen

Luncheon at Brompton Court went off without a hitch despite the chaotic preparations. The landscapers had outdone themselves. The smell of freshly cut grass hung over the garden, the moss-free duck pond sparkled invitingly as the newly scrubbed nymph tossed her bucket of water into its mesmerizing depths and the pale façade of the house shimmered in the midday sun.

"It's gorgeous," breathed Mimi as the limousine drove through the gates and up the winding path.

Donna simply stared, utterly entranced. Daisy winked at Floria. Brompton Court had that effect on one.

They entered through the front entrance, which bore no resemblance to the crime scene it was only a few days ago. The giant crystal chandelier, polished to perfection by a team of experts, glittered above their heads, while the marble floor sparkled beguilingly. All traces of Serena's blood and the forensic markers had been thoroughly removed.

Floria, true to form, had planned everything to perfection. The table setting could have been photographed for a decor magazine, it was so tastefully decorated. Several short, glass vases each holding a single white rose and a bunch of white freesias were positioned along the center of the table on a white linen runner shot through with silver thread. In between the vases were thin, tapered candles, unlit, but providing a cool, understated elegance. Violeta had brought out the fine bone china cutlery, and the cut glass wineglasses perfected the picture.

The lamb shanks were mouthwateringly tender and served with Moroccan couscous and a light, green salad. The chilled chardonnay, which Daisy always thought tasted better in cut glass, went a long way to help steady their collective nerves. Floria, buoyed up by adrenaline, kept up a constant flow of conversation, helped along by Daisy, who tried to draw out the sisters a bit.

Donna was the first to open up. She seemed more at ease now it was just the four of them, plus Daisy. Sir Ranulph had opted to eat in his room, announcing that he was fatigued by the service and wanted to rest before the hordes arrived for the reception at three o'clock.

"That was a lovely ceremony. Thanks, Floria, for organizing. It must have been a lot of work." Donna had a delightfully soft Austrian accent.

"I was happy to do it," beamed Floria. The others may have thought she was being modest, but Daisy knew how much she loved organizing events, and she had a real flair for it too.

"You played really well," Mimi told Donna, who blushed.

"I was so nervous. I was petrified of making a mistake in front of all those people."

"I thought you did marvelously well," said Daisy, and she meant it. Ten years of piano lessons and endless practice hours hadn't cultivated the raw talent she recognized in Donna.

Donna smiled. "Thank you."

"I did feel a bit like a piece of meat," said Mimi in her Australian accent, poking her lamb with her fork. "Everyone was gawking at us, like we were from another planet. I saw several people take photographs with their phones. What's all that about?"

"That is Serena's legacy, I'm afraid." Floria sighed. "You were a secret for so long; now your identities have been revealed, everyone wants to know who you are and what you look like. I'd be surprised if the press don't start contacting you for interviews."

"Heavens," whispered Donna, appalled. "I don't think I'd like that."

Daisy could see she was a very private person, and the notion of being in the papers scared her to death. "You can always say no," she said gently.

"Serena was extremely well-known," Floria tried to explain. "I've grown up in her shadow, so I don't notice it as much anymore, but it is tiresome having people, particularly the press, judge your every move and criticize you for staying out too late or drinking too much."

Daisy knew she was talking from experience. Floria had a long history with the press, thanks to her mother's fame. In the eyes of the media, she was the spoiled rich girl, Serena's wild child who acted out for attention. While there might have been some grain of truth in that label at one stage, Floria had moved on and was nowhere near as wild as her reputation suggested. Still, none of her half sisters knew that.

"Why, just last month one of the tabloids posted a

picture of Daisy and me frolicking in a Jacuzzi, and my boyfriend dumped me because he said it made him look bad."

"What? He dumped you because of that?" Mimi stared at her uncomprehendingly. "My boyfriend dumped me because I hit him across the stage during a concert."

Daisy laughed. The more she got to know Mimi, the more she liked her. "See, I told you James was an asshole," she said to Floria, who couldn't help but grin.

"I can't match that," she acknowledged, "but I was really hurt. I felt like the press had destroyed my life."

"It sounds like you'd be better off without him." Mimi sniffed.

"Hear hear," echoed Daisy, raising her glass.

"It's always going to be like that," spat Carmen, who hadn't said a word up until now. Her plate lay untouched in front of her. Her glass, however, had been refilled three times.

"Now that *she's* dead, we're not going to get a moment's peace. The press will always be breathing down our necks."

"Do you think so?" Donna stared at her as the reality of the situation dawned.

"It's not all bad," said Floria hurriedly. "Serena had a lot of useful connections that will come in handy if you're in the music industry, which you all are." She glanced pointedly at Donna. "I know you said you played in an orchestra in Vienna, but if, for example, you wanted to move to England, I could hook you up with some contacts and have you working in no time." She turned to Carmen. "And you already attracted a lot of attention after your aria in the church. That's all because of who Serena was."

Carmen snorted but knew better than to respond. An

uncomfortable silence hung over the table as the sisters got to grips with their new reality.

"I'll be jetting back to Sydney soon, so I don't care," said Mimi with a nonchalant shrug of her shoulders. "We have heard about Dame Serena over there, but I doubt anyone will recognize me. Besides, I plan to give myself a makeover before I go back, so hopefully I'll be incognito, at least until I get my singing career up and running again."

"Oh, if you're having a makeover, you must let Daisy style your hair," cried Floria, diluting the tension with one expertly delivered sentence. "She's a genius."

Mimi looked uncertain.

"I own a hair salon." Daisy smiled reassuringly. She studied Mimi's rather wild, dark hair. "I'm thinking an edgy French cut with a fringe. It's very now, perfect for a bourgeoning pop star."

Mimi thought about it, then broke into a grin. "I can see that working. Let's give it a try."

"Great!" Floria refilled all their glasses. "I'd like to make a toast. Here's to Serena, who was a terrible mother, but did one good thing by bringing us all together."

DI McGuinness came around at a respectable two o'-clock, an hour before the guests were due to arrive for the memorial reception. Everything was ready. Tables containing a delectable range of canapés had been set up in the parlor, a large, spacious room that had doubled as a ballroom or a disco when Serena had been alive. Her parties had been legendary, and many of the guests coming this afternoon would have some wild stories to tell. Caterers had been coming and going all morning; Nellie, the florist, had done a magnificent job with the flower arrangements; and Sam, a technician friend of Floria who'd done the electronics at the memorial service, had set up a microphone for the speeches and the music system, which was set to play all of Serena's songs on repeat.

Violeta showed him into the living room, where Floria was regaling her sisters with stories about Serena: her wonderful career and her tumultuous personal life. Daisy, who'd heard most of the anecdotes before, relaxed in an armchair and studied their body language while marveling at the differences in their personalities.

Floria, as usual, commanded the room. She had them in stitches one minute and staring at her in horror the next; but then, Serena's antics did have that effect on one. Only Carmen was unmoved. She kept glancing at the door like she wanted to escape through it, but because she was obliged to stay until the will had been read, she was trapped.

"It's a nightmare," Daisy heard her whispering into her phone after lunch. "I don't want to know how rich she was or how wonderful her life was. I'm glad she's dead."

Donna was quiet and reserved, although clearly emotional at being reunited with her sisters. She said very little about her life in Austria, other than that she played in an orchestra. She was definitely more of a listener than a talker. Perhaps she felt her life was dull compared to theirs. There was a sadness in her eyes, and Daisy remembered Paul saying he thought she'd been crying. Maybe there was something else bothering her other than Serena's death and the sisters' subsequent reunion.

Mimi, on the other hand, was a firebrand and couldn't be more different from her twin sister. She didn't hold back and angrily told them the reason she'd sent her boyfriend flying was because he'd been cheating on her with the lead guitarist, a slutty girl called Lilith. "He's welcome to her," she hissed, clearly not over him. "She'll shag anything that moves."

"Just like her namesake," murmured Floria, who'd studied the classics. At Mimi's dark look she hurried to add, "She was a mythical creature representing ungodliness and chaos." She left off "and seduction."

"Sounds about right," huffed Mimi.

"Hello, Inspector," Daisy said as Paul entered the room. He wore the same smart trousers as he had at the church minus the jacket, with his sleeves rolled up and a determined expression on his face. Casual yet authoritative. Floria stopped talking, and all three sisters turned toward him. He cleared his throat. "I'm sorry to interrupt your reunion, but would it be all right if I asked the girls a few questions?"

"I am not being interrogated." Carmen jumped up. "I know my rights."

"I'm afraid you have no choice, Miss Vega. If you refuse, I'll have to arrest you and take you to the police station, where we'll conduct the interview in more formal surroundings."

Donna gasped.

Carmen glared at him but sat down.

If looks could kill, thought Daisy.

"They weren't even in the country when Serena was murdered," said Floria's friend Greg, the solicitor who was also executor of Serena's will. He'd just arrived and cut a dashing figure in a dove-gray suit with a crisp white shirt underneath. It went well with his dark, blond hair and intelligent blue eyes. Daisy noticed Donna suddenly perk up. "What bearing could they possibly have on the case?"

Daisy got to her feet and stood beside Paul in a show of support. "It's just routine, Greg. Don't get your legal knickers in a twist."

Greg rolled his eyes at her, then smiled at everybody else. "Glad to see you're all getting on."

"Daisy will sit in on the interviews," Paul announced, gazing around the room, daring anyone to contradict him. "That way it won't be so intimidating."

"Putting your studies to good use, Daisy?" Greg grinned, glancing from her to the detective and back again. She shot him a warning glance. Mimi and Donna both nodded, happy with that. Carmen sat stony-faced, saying nothing.

"Who wants to go first?" asked Paul.

"I will," said Mimi, uncurling from the couch and stretching like a cat. "May as well get it over with."

Daisy glanced at Floria. "Can we use the library?" It wasn't so much a library as a game room, complete with a billiards and a poker table and a fully stocked bar. Daisy had spent many a debauched night in there with Floria and her friends. It was a warm, comforting room, not intimidating in the slightest, which would help to relax the girls.

"Of course."

Daisy led the way, Paul on her heels and Mimi a few steps behind.

"Wow, I'll bet you've had some fun times in here." Mimi took in the ornately curved bar at one end, the full-size billiard table in the center and the card tables at the other end. A compact, digital sound system sat on a narrow table beneath the window with a small but powerful speaker positioned next to it. An open dartboard cabinet hung on the opposite wall under which the snooker cues were stacked in a custom-made rack. A fluorescent billiard table light on two chains hung above the table, but it was off. Daisy laughed and turned on a light above the bar. "You bet." She pointed to the poker table. "Shall we?"

Paul nodded, and they sat down. He took out a small, leather-bound notepad and a pen, and looked at Mimi. "I understand your surname is Turner, is that correct?"

Mimi nodded. "That's my adopted surname, the name on my passport."

Paul nodded. "It's just so I get it straight."

Daisy smiled at her. "How did you react when Greg called you out of the blue and told you about Serena?"

Mimi's shoulders stiffened. "I was shocked. I had no idea I was adopted, let alone by a famous opera singer. I confronted my mother, who admitted it was true. We had the most awful row."

Daisy grimaced sympathetically. "I'm sorry to hear that. Do you think your mother had a reason for not telling you?"

"If she did, she didn't say what it was." Mimi's expression turned sullen. "I'm not sure I can forgive her for lying to me all these years."

"I'm sure she only did what she thought was best." Daisy glanced at Paul, who gave her a little nod. He was happy to let her continue for the moment. He wasn't interviewing the girls under caution; it was merely to rule them out as suspects.

Mimi grunted. "You know, I had a long time to think

about things on the flight over here, and it's all starting to make sense."

"What is?" Daisy asked.

"Why I'm so different from my parents. They were both teachers, quiet and studious. They never made a fuss about anything. I was the one who was always acting up, the one who didn't play by the rules. My father tried to discipline me, but it only made things worse. I rebelled, got into the wrong crowd, became even more wild." She lowered her head. "Until he gave up on me. I was a huge disappointment to him."

"What about your mother?" Daisy prompted, feeling sorry for Mimi. It was clear she had inherited Serena's drive and spirit, the two qualities that had been instrumental in her becoming a star but could be difficult in an unhappy teenager.

"Mother never contradicted him, although I suppose in her own way she tried to help me. She used to call me every week, knowing I'd rarely pick up. She'd offer me money, which I never took."

"It sounds like she really cared for you."

Mimi gazed at her, her eyes hard. "You'd think so, but then she kept this hidden from me my whole life when it would have helped me understand why I was so different."

"So your parents are still alive?" The question came from Paul, who'd been studying Mimi intently.

"My father passed away several years ago, but my mother's still alive."

He nodded, then changed tack. "Can you confirm which flight you took to London?"

Mimi frowned. "I can't remember the actual flight number, but it was Qantas Airways and it left Wednesday night from Sydney airport. I have the boarding pass in my bag somewhere; if you'd like to see it?"

"That won't be necessary, thank you." He already knew which flight she'd been on; he was just checking. Besides, he'd seen her get off the plane at Heathrow. "Just one more thing: Did you know about the Modigliani?"

"The painting? No. Floria told us it was stolen the night Serena was killed, but prior to that I didn't know it existed."

He nodded, then glanced at Daisy. "Anything else?"

She shook her head. "No, I think that's it. Thanks, Mimi. You've been very helpful. I'm sorry all this has opened such a can of worms for you back home."

Mimi shrugged. "At least I know now." Then she got up and stalked out of the room.

Donna was next. She poked her head around the door and tentatively asked, "Can I come in?"

"Please do." Daisy gestured to the chair Mimi had vacated.

Donna gingerly sat down. It was clear she was very nervous, despite the fact she had nothing to be nervous about. "I—I'm sorry, I've never been interviewed by the police before," she stammered, casting furtive glances at DI McGuinness, who didn't do anything to lessen her discomfort.

"Don't worry, it's just routine." Daisy gave her a bright smile and saw her slender shoulders relax. She really was very uptight.

"What's your full name?" asked Paul, following the same procedure as before.

"Donna Brunner."

"And you live in Kitzbühel, Austria, is that right?"

"No, I was born in Kitzbühel—that's where my parents live, but I stay in Vienna."

"Ah." Paul made a note on his pad.

"Vienna is a beautiful city," said Daisy. "I went to the opera there once."

Paul raised an eyebrow but didn't speak.

"Oh yes, we have a fabulous opera theater," said Donna, her eyes lighting up now she was on familiar ground. "We have all the best stars come and sing for us; in fact, I'm sure Serena Levanté came once. I remember seeing her face on a poster. Of course, I had no idea . . . " Her voice faded off.

Daisy smiled sympathetically. "You couldn't have known."

"But you were aware you were adopted?" Paul leaned back in his chair and folded his arms across his chest.

"Oh yes. My parents never made a secret of it. But like I said before, we didn't make the connection with Serena Levanté because she wasn't known by that name when she gave birth to us."

"Do you know what name she went by?" asked Paul.

Donna thought for a moment. "Edith Humphries—that was it. My mother fished out the birth certificate before I flew to London. I have it with me somewhere."

"God, no wonder she changed it," blurted out Daisy, earning her a stern look from Paul.

Donna giggled. "It's awful, isn't it?"

"So, where were you when Mr. Edwards called and told you the news?" Paul asked, trying to get the conversation back on track.

The light went out of Donna's eyes. "I was at home. I live with my boyfriend, Hans, the director of the orchestra

I play in, but we broke up shortly after I got the call from Greg, I mean, Mr. Edwards."

"Not because of the news, I hope?" Daisy looked alarmed.

"Oh no, nothing like that." She hesitated, uncertain as to whether she ought to continue.

"So what happened?" urged Daisy. She sensed this was important.

Donna sighed. "Hans wasn't home when I got the call, but I was so excited, I wanted to pack immediately, then stop at my parents' house before going to the airport. So I got down a suitcase from on top of the cupboard, and inside I found the rental agreement for our flat." She stared into her lap and her back curled like she wished the chair would swallow her whole. "He must have hidden it there."

"Why is that such a bad thing?" Daisy struggled to see the relevance.

"It's so shameful," whispered Donna, tears coming into her eyes.

Daisy reached for her hand across the table. "It's okay. We aren't here to judge you. We just need to know the truth. I could see you were upset, but DI McGuinness needs to know why, else he might think you were involved in Serena's death."

Paul nodded in agreement.

Donna gasped. "No, it's nothing like that."

"Then tell us," said Daisy. "What was the significance of the lease?"

"The rent was being paid by Hans's wife." She hung her head in shame. "Our apartment was in her name. He's separated and we were engaged to be married. He even gave me a ring." She stared at the ring finger on her left hand, now conspicuously bare. "Hans was going to divorce his wife, except when I confronted him about the lease, he admitted she holds the purse strings and funds the orchestra—his orchestra—so there's no way he'd ever divorce her." Her eyes pleaded with them to understand.

"It's okay, Donna. We all make mistakes. You weren't to know."

Donna dropped her head into her hands. "I feel like such a fool. All the time we were together, he never intended to divorce his wife."

Paul rubbed his forehead. It was clear that Donna had had nothing at all to do with Serena's murder. She had been dealing with her own crisis back in Austria, and that was the reason she was so upset.

"Listen, we've all been there," said Daisy soothingly. "My boyfriend walked out on me a couple of years back without so much as a warning. Floria was dumped only last week. Serena had four husbands, for goodness' sake. It happens."

She felt Paul's eyes on her.

"I suppose so," sniffed Donna, trying to pull herself together. "It's just such a terrible cliché."

Daisy stood up and walked around the table to put an arm round Donna's shoulders. "Come on, let's go get you another glass of bubbly."

It was Carmen's turn next. The opera singer sat stiffly at the table, her hands in her lap, staring straight in front of her.

Daisy opened her mouth, but Paul surprised her by holding up a hand.

"I've got this one."

Daisy nodded and sat back. She didn't envy him. Carmen would be a tough nut to crack.

"What is your full name?" His voice was clipped and to the point.

"Carmen Vega."

"So, Serena took your father's name, even though they weren't married?"

"At least it was good for something." Carmen scowled. "She could take his name, but not his child."

Paul met Daisy's eye. Carmen was filled with bitterness, and it was clear she hated her birth mother. But was she capable of murder?

"Where were you the night Serena Levanté was murdered?" asked Paul.

Carmen gave an arrogant toss of her head. "I was in Barcelona, of course. You know this."

"Can anyone vouch for you?"

"My boyfriend, Pedro. I was with him."

Paul nodded and opened a file on the table. Inside was a printout that he slid across the table toward her. "This is a passenger list compliments of easyJet. It says here that your boyfriend Pedro was in London last weekend. He arrived on the Friday morning and flew back to Barcelona on the Sunday night."

A heavy silence descended on them.

Daisy stared at Paul, then Carmen, who'd paled perceptibly. He'd certainly kept that one close to his chest.

Eventually, Carmen whispered, "Then I was alone."

"Well, which was it, Carmen? Were you alone or were you with Pedro?"

She glared at him. "I was alone."

He stared back at her, his steely eyes unwavering.

Daisy could see why he was good at interrogations. He knew just how to intimidate his suspect.

"Are you sure you wouldn't like to change your story? I should remind you that lying to a police officer is a criminal offense. You wouldn't want to jeopardize your singing career before it even got started, now would you?"

She swallowed, the reality of her situation sinking in. After a long moment she sighed and said, "Okay, I was in London too."

Daisy inhaled sharply. So she had been here when Serena was murdered. This put a new spin on things. She had to admit Paul was tough, but he got results.

"Could you be more specific? When exactly did you arrive and why were you here?"

Carmen stretched her neck to the side, as if she was straining to leave the room. "It's personal."

Paul raised his voice a notch. "I don't think you understand how serious this is, Carmen. You were in London the night of your mother's murder and you have given us no alibi. Everyone knows you hated Serena and you will probably inherit from her will, which means you had ample motive. So if I were you, I'd start talking."

"I didn't kill that woman," spat Carmen.

"Then tell us why you were here," begged Daisy.

She studied Carmen's face, the hard, green eyes angled down into her lap, the permanent scowl on her otherwise flawless brow, and how she fiddled with a small gold ring on her right hand.

"Was it because of Pedro?"

Carmen's eyes flickered.

Bingo, thought Daisy. "Did you come to be with him?"

Carmen tossed back her head and said with much disdain, "I came to see if he was with anyone."

"You mean another woman?" Paul frowned.

Carmen leaned forward and hissed at him. "Yes, of course another woman. Who else do you think he'd be with? A man, maybe? I can assure you Pedro is not gay."

"That is not what I meant." Paul's eyes burned with an intensity Daisy hadn't seen before, but he kept his tone even. She had to admire his control, but then, she supposed he was used to interrogating violent criminals. Compared to that, Carmen must be a walk in the park. Still, the two glared at each other across the table.

"And was he?" whispered Daisy, hoping to dissipate the sudden tension. "Was he having an affair?"

Carmen turned her blazing gaze onto her. "No, he was alone." The satisfied smirk told Daisy she was telling the truth.

Paul glanced down at his notes. "So, you didn't come anywhere near Brompton Court on Saturday night?"

"No," Carmen sneered. "I was with Pedro all night. We had dinner at the Hard Rock Cafe and then returned to the hotel."

"And Pedro will vouch for you, will he?" asked Paul.

"Of course."

Once she'd left the room, Daisy confronted him, "You are a very sneaky man, Paul McGuinness. You knew she'd been in London all along, didn't you?"

He tried to prevent a grin but couldn't quite manage it. "I checked to see whether Carmen or Donna had been on any flights the weekend Serena was killed, and there it was in black and white. Carmen Vega flew into Gatwick at three o'clock on Saturday afternoon and left on Sunday evening, on the same flight as her boyfriend. I was immediately suspicious, but I didn't want to jump to any conclusions until I'd spoken to her. Just as well, seeing as her visit had nothing to do with Serena's death."

"But she had opportunity and motive, and just between you and me, she also has the temperament. It wouldn't have been hard to catch a train or taxi to Edgemead, walk to Brompton Court—there's a path through the woods from the station—murder Serena, then return to Edgemead and catch a taxi back to her hotel."

In fact, in her mind's eye, Daisy could imagine Carmen wielding a heavy object and smashing it down on poor Serena's head. She couldn't get the disturbing thought out of her head.

"Except I checked with the hotel. They had a reservation at the Hard Rock Cafe, as she said. According to the night manager, they got back around eleven on Saturday evening and didn't leave their room until the following morning."

"Okay, so she was telling the truth. She really did come to London to check up on her boyfriend."

He nodded. "It would seem so."

Chapter Seventeen

The reception was in full swing when Krish, Penny and Asa arrived. They'd worked that morning because Friday was one of their busiest days of the week, but now the salon was shut and, as a treat, Floria had invited them to the reception.

Daisy met them outside. "Did you have a busy morning?"

"Frantic," gushed Krish, gazing in awe at the four-pillared portico that stood at the entrance to the house. "Mrs. Halliard came in with bright-green hair because she peroxided it in Spain, then went swimming in the hotel pool. So we had to juggle several customers at once until we'd sorted her out."

The front doors were wide open and several guests stood outside, smoking and admiring the view. Brompton Court was built on a small mound, so one could look out across the wooded valley and over the village of Edgemead, which lay nestled beyond, its steeple just visible above the treeline.

"It's gorgeous," breathed Asa, staring up at the

shimmering stone façade. "I had no idea it was so massive. My entire apartment block could fit in here."

They walked up the stone steps and went inside. Niall Barclay, husband number two, stood in the hallway, chatting up a pretty brunette.

"Hello, Niall." Daisy gave him a knowing look.

He grinned. "Hello, Daisy darling. Lovely to see you again. You are looking well." His eyes roamed over her body, then shifted to Penny, who'd followed her in. In his midfifties, Niall had lost none of the charismatic Irish charm that had attracted Serena's attention and made him one of the most successful horse breeders in the country.

"Wow, is he taken?" Krish's eyes were popping out of his head.

"He's an incorrigible womanizer, Krish dear. Not really your type."

"Pity." Krish followed Daisy into the parlor, where alcohol was being served, along with a vast table of canapés.

"Oh good, I'm starving," said Asa, dashing off to fill a plate with goodies.

"I think I'll get a drink." Penny headed in the direction of the bar. "Are you coming, Krish?"

Floria rushed over, her lips pressed together in fury.

"What's the matter?" Daisy asked. Her friend had been so upbeat after the memorial service.

She took a shallow, angry breath. "I've just caught that bastard Collin pitching Brompton Court to some Texas billionaire like it's a foregone conclusion he's going to inherit the place. Can you believe the audacity of the man?"

"It's a bit premature, isn't it?" Daisy wondered if something had happened that she didn't know about.

"Exactly." Floria frowned. "You don't think he knows

what's in the will, do you? Oh, Daisy. I'll die if I lose this place. It's my childhood home."

"Let's not count our chickens, okay? Not until the will is read and we know for sure who's going to inherit the mansion." She glanced around. "Speaking of the will, where is Greg?"

"He's prepping, most likely. We're going to adjourn to the dining room to read it in a minute. It's immediate family only, I'm afraid, although your detective has insisted on being present."

"That's okay," said Daisy, vaguely disgruntled, not because she needed to be there, but because she was dying to see if Serena had left anyone with a big enough motive to kill her. Paul would no doubt inform her of the outcome later. She patted Floria's hand. "You can tell me all about it afterward."

After the family disappeared into the dining room, Daisy decided to fill in the gaps in their investigation by talking to Serena's exes. Niall, she already knew, had been in Argentina at the time of the murder, so he couldn't have stolen the painting or killed Serena. Hubert, Serena's third husband, a respected antique furniture dealer with one store in Notting Hill and another in Paris, was stuffing a vol-au-vent into his mouth when Daisy approached.

"How's the antique business, Hubert?"

He chewed frantically before clearing his throat. "Going through a bit of a slump at the moment actually, Daisy. How are things at your salon?"

Hubert was one of their few male customers, despite not living in the area. The barber at the other end of the High Street did most of the men in town, but Hubert, being fabulously gay, loved the glamour and the free prosecco he got at Ooh La La. Daisy remembered Floria saying he'd signed a prenup when he married Serena—Greg had insisted on it—so when they got divorced he'd only received a small settlement. If his business was in trouble, that might provide a motive for stealing the painting. She studied him, taking in the slightly chubby face with mottled cheeks, no doubt from too many late-night sherries in front of the fire. But his expression was open and he radiated an energy and excitement for life that was contagious. No, she doubted very much Hubert had stolen the painting, even though it had to have been someone with an intimate knowledge of Brompton Court.

"Did you know the Modigliani is back?" She wanted to gauge his reaction. She'd seen the forensic van pull up an hour before.

"Really?" He perked up. "Where is it? I haven't seen it for a while. Shall we have a naughty little peek?"

Daisy wasn't expecting that, but she nodded. It would be interesting to see his expression when faced with the painting. "I believe it's in Collin's study."

They snuck up the grand staircase and across the landing to the study. Hubert gazed up at the painting of Serena and shivered. "I can't help but feel she's still here, looking down on us."

"It does have that effect on one," agreed Daisy. She'd felt it many times before as well. The eyes of the painting seemed to follow you as you walked across the landing. The study door was unlocked and they went in. The Modigliani lay on the desk, unwrapped.

Daisy turned on the desk lamp so they could have a better look. It really was exquisite. Hubert stared at it, enraptured. "I've never seen it this close before." She watched his eyes follow the pale face of the woman in the painting, then move down her slender neck and finally hover over her dark clothing. Suddenly, he frowned.

"What is it?" Daisy asked.

He bent over the painting and stared at the golden signature mark for a long time before straightening his back. "I thought it was damaged just there over the signature, but I see now I was mistaken. It's in pristine condition."

"We'd better go before anyone finds us here." Daisy didn't think Collin would take too kindly to them ogling his beloved Modigliani. Luckily, he was still in the dining room with the others and would be for another half hour at least.

Hubert nodded, and together they left the study and went back downstairs.

Daisy found Niall chatting up Penny, who looked stunning in a floor-length black gown with tiny, spaghetti straps that showed off her elegant shoulders. Her mass of fiery red hair was up in a loose bun, with tendrils caressing her neck.

"Mind if I join you?" she asked, perching on a vacant seat. Niall, ever the gentleman, looked up and smiled. "Of course, Daisy. I was disappointed not to see you or Floria at Ascot this year. Bartered Bride won first place in the Gold Cup."

"I heard. Congratulations. So, things are going well, then?"

He gave the sort of arrogant shrug that very wealthy men can afford to give. "It's a competitive industry, but we do okay."

He was playing it down. Daisy knew he'd done exceptionally well these past few years. She remembered watching an episode of *Countryfile*, on which they'd discussed how his stud farm had more than doubled in size, now taking up a sizable portion of the Surrey countryside. Out of all Serena's ex-husbands, he was least likely to murder her. He didn't need the money and, as far as she knew, they hadn't parted on bad terms. In fact, according to Greg, Serena divorcing him had given him the capital he'd needed to upgrade his farm.

He changed the subject. "You know, I'm not surprised Serena died surrounded by mystery. She always had a flare for the dramatic. Why should her death be any different?"

Daisy chuckled. "It's true, and she would have loved all this attention."

Niall rolled his eyes. "Aye, that she would. I don't miss it, I can tell you. My life has quietened down considerably since we split up, and my blood pressure has reverted to normal again."

"It wasn't that long ago, really, was it?" asked Daisy, trying to remember in which order the husbands came. Sir Ranulph was first, with Floria being born almost immediately. Their marriage had lasted fifteen years, and the resulting stability was largely responsible for Serena's meteoric rise to fame. A string of lovers followed, which, according to Floria, made Serena more highly strung than ever, until she met Niall and settled down again, albeit briefly, before cheating on him with a handsome cellist in the London Symphony Orchestra. Her relationship with Hubert was fleeting, and probably born out of a desperate need to be looked after rather than loved.

"We divorced eight years ago," he said after a moment's reflection. "We had some grand times, though. When we met she was at the height of her career. It was dazzling. We traveled extensively, met celebrities and royalty, and lived in five-star hotels around the world. It was a whirlwind existence." His eyes got a faraway look in them, and Daisy was glad at least one person had some fond memories of Serena. "We were very much in love." He glanced at them, then added dryly, "Well, I was very much in love. For Serena, I suspect it was more lust. The only true love she ever had was her singing."

It wasn't the first time Daisy had heard that said.

"It sounds so glamorous." Penny gazed up at him, clearly infatuated. Daisy hoped she wasn't going to fall for the womanizing horse breeder. As charming as Niall was, he was lethal with women. Daisy made a mental note to have a serious talk with Penny on Monday.

Floria, Mimi and Donna burst into the parlor and made straight for the bar. The reading of the will must be over.

"If you'll excuse me." Daisy stood up. She couldn't wait to hear what the outcome was.

"We're celebrating, Daisy," sang Floria, asking for a bottle of champagne. "Serena was surprisingly altruistic and split everything equally between her four daughters."

"Given her vast fortune, that is a considerable amount," added Greg, joining them at the makeshift bar.

"Really? That's great news. I'm so happy for you all."

"It was very unexpected," said Donna, whose hand was shaking as she accepted her drink. Daisy imagined this would make all the difference to the professional violinist. "You don't have to go back to Austria now. You could stay in England and start over."

"Yes, it opens so many doors." Donna's eyes glazed

over as she considered the possibilities. Greg smiled at her. It was clear he wanted her to stay.

"You're telling me," gushed Mimi, her eyes bright. "I'm going to use the money to launch my singing career. Voice training, dance coaching, a complete makeover. I'll show that bastard Kyle that I don't need his poxy band to be successful."

"The Australian Taylor Swift," Floria said proudly.

Mimi grinned. "You got it!"

Their excitement was contagious.

"Where's Carmen?" asked Daisy.

Floria's face fell. "She's signing some documents, but then she's going to leave. She really is very bitter."

Mimi leaned forward and whispered conspiratorially, "She said it was the least the bitch could do."

"Her behavior is quite shocking," remarked Donna. Greg put a hand on her back. "She harbors great animosity toward Serena for abandoning her."

"I assume she was provided for?" Daisy wondered if Carmen had had a rough childhood, which would magnify her resentment.

Greg shrugged. "If she was, it wasn't handled by my firm."

"We certainly weren't provided for in any way, shape or form," scoffed Mimi. "So I don't imagine she was either."

"No, that's true," mused Daisy.

Floria took a gulp of her champagne. "It must be hard for her to see me at Brompton Court and think that this is the upbringing she should have had. She is the eldest, after all. Perhaps that's why she hates me so much."

"I think she hates everyone," cut in Mimi.

Daisy thought Floria might have a point. Carmen's hatred of Serena had been years and years in the making. She must have had a very tough childhood to be harboring that level of bitterness, even now, in her thirties.

"Perhaps you could look into it for us, Greg?" asked Daisy.

"You mean for the purposes of the investigation?" He frowned. "I'm not sure DI McGuinness would approve."

"It's got nothing to do with the investigation," Daisy assured him. "Carmen's already been cleared as a suspect. It's just that we might understand her better if we found out a bit about her background."

"I'm with Daisy on this one," agreed Floria. "It would be nice to know a bit more about her, because she's not at all forthcoming."

"I wouldn't bother." Mimi sniffed. "If she doesn't want to open up, that's her problem. We don't need her."

"I feel sorry for her." Donna took a sip from her flute.

"I wouldn't," scoffed Mimi, giving her twin a dark look. "Did you hear her sing at the memorial service? She's going to be a star in no time. She won't need Serena's money. Being her illegitimate daughter was enough to get her noticed."

Angry voices in the entrance hall interrupted their discussion.

"That sounds like Hubert." Floria shook her head in confusion. "I've never heard him raise his voice before."

There was a loud smash as something crashed onto the marbled floor, followed closely by a man's voice crying out.

They all dashed into the hall to see what was going on.

Chapter Eighteen

In the hallway, they found Hubert up against the wall with Collin's hands around his neck. Hubert's face was an alarming shade of purple.

"Collin, what are you doing?" cried Floria, running forward. "Let him go immediately!"

"What's the meaning of this?" barked Paul, emerging from down the hall.

"He's lying!" growled Collin, dropping his hands from Hubert's neck, but glaring at the antique dealer like he wanted to continue throttling him.

"You're the liar," sneered Hubert in a rare show of animosity. "What do you think we are? Fools?"

The two men glared at each other until Paul said, "Okay, that's enough. Everyone, calm down."

"I'm sorry, Floria." Hubert flounced past her and out into the garden. "I need some air."

Collin hissed something under his breath.

"That'll be quite enough, thank you," Paul warned him. The guests who'd crowded into the hallway to watch the fireworks now trickled back into the parlor, talking among themselves.

"What was that all about?" Paul asked Collin once the hallway was clear.

Collin was still seething. "Hubert had the gall to tell me the Modigliani was a fake. It's a preposterous notion. It's been authenticated by Sotheby's. The man is off his rocker."

"And you're sure this is the same painting you acquired?" asked Daisy.

"Are you thinking it might have been switched for a fake during the robbery?" Paul glanced at her. The inspector had followed her line of thought perfectly.

She shrugged. "It's a theory."

"No way." Collin was adamant. "I inspected it when it was returned from the lab. It's definitely the original. I'd have known if it was a fake. This is what I do for a living, for God's sake."

Paul held up a hand. "Okay, I'll take your word for it. Why don't you go get a drink and try to calm down? And stay away from Hubert."

Collin gave a stiff nod and marched off, shaking his head.

"There's never a dull moment around here, is there?" Paul stared after Collin's departing figure.

"Not as long as I've known Floria," replied Daisy with a grin. "But seriously, I've never seen Hubert that angry before. Collin must really have got his back up."

"He did almost strangle him," pointed out Paul. "That would piss me off too."

Daisy steered him outside onto the portico for some privacy. "So, what happened at the reading of the will? Who inherited Brompton Court? I've been dying to know."

Paul chuckled. "That was a surprise. It went to Sir Ranulph, to revert to Floria on his death. Collin was quite put out. He didn't get a thing."

"Really? That is interesting."

Collin had obviously thought he'd inherit the country pile if he'd been showing it off to the Texas billionaire, but the fact that he'd got nothing meant that it couldn't be him Serena had been thinking of cutting out of her will.

"So, it wasn't him Serena was talking about when she mentioned she didn't owe anyone any favors." Paul had read her mind again.

"It must have been one of the girls, then."

"Or all of them," Paul interjected. "The housekeeper and her husband got a modest amount. It was enough to buy a property, but nothing to write home about. Besides, I can't see Serena wanting to cut them out of the will."

"Not after everything they've done for her over the years," said Daisy. "They've been such loyal servants."

"Unless something happened that we don't know about," mused Paul.

"Let's ask Collin," said Daisy, turning around and heading indoors toward the library. "He's probably drowning his sorrows."

"You're not going to have another go at me, are you?" They found Collin sitting at the bar, staring into a glass of scotch.

"No, it's not about the painting." Daisy perched on a barstool next to him.

"Oh?"

"It's about Violeta," said Paul. "Do you know of any

reason Serena might have wanted to cut her out of her will?"

Collin's forehead furrowed. "Cut her out of the will? But she didn't. They were awarded a substantial amount. More than I bloody got."

"No, but we think she may have been considering it," said Daisy.

"Really? Well, I didn't know anything about that."

"They didn't have any fights or arguments recently, anything that you remember?"

Collin shook his head. "I don't recall anything. Violeta wouldn't dare argue with Serena. Nor would most people, for that matter."

"I believe Serena threw a glass after you left on Saturday."

"Really? I didn't know."

"Okay, thanks anyway," said Paul, turning away. That was clearly a dead end. Collin didn't know anything.

"Actually, now that you mention it, I did once see Serena arguing with Pepe, Violeta's husband, in the garden."

"When was this?" asked Daisy.

"About a month ago. I was coming up the driveway when I saw them standing next to the duck pond. They were deep in conversation and didn't notice me. Pepe seemed to be pleading with her, but she wasn't having any of it, and she stormed off into the rose garden. I don't know what they were discussing, but it looked to be important."

"I think we'd better have a word with Pepe," said Paul. They found him in the kitchen, sitting at the table drinking a cup of coffee while Violeta loaded the dish-washer for the umpteenth time.

"Might we have a word, Mr. Bonello?" Paul asked.

Pepe looked up and nodded.

They took a seat opposite him.

"What's this about, Daisy?" Violeta glanced at her with worried eyes.

"Nothing to be concerned about, Violeta. DI McGuinness just wants to ask Pepe a few questions."

Pepe put down his mug, and Daisy could see by the way he held it how crippled with arthritis his hands were.

"We believe you had an argument with Serena a few weeks before her death," Paul began. Pepe looked confused. "I don't know what you mean."

"In the garden," Daisy said. "By the duck pond. You were seen having a heated discussion before Serena marched off into the rose garden."

"Oh, that." He shook his head, as if he didn't want to talk about it.

"It's important you tell us what it was about, Pepe," said Paul, his eyes boring into the old man.

"It isn't my place to say," mumbled Pepe, looking to his wife for assurance.

Violeta sighed. "I don't suppose it matters now that she's dead. You'd better tell them, Pepe."

Daisy looked from Violeta to Pepe. Clearly, there was something they were covering up.

Pepe looked at his hands, then the table and finally out the kitchen window. Anywhere but at the inspector. Eventually, he said, "I promised Serena I wouldn't ever talk about it again."

It was sounding more and more mysterious by the

second. Paul was getting impatient. "Please, tell us what you know."

He sighed. "It happened about a month ago. I was about to go to bed when I remembered I hadn't put away the tractor. April showers and all that. So I got up and walked across the lawn to where it was parked. It was then that I saw her."

"Who?" asked Daisy.

"Serena. She was floating across the lawn like a ghost. I swear, I thought I was seeing things. Then she collapsed by the duck pond. I ran over to her, and for a minute I thought she was dead. She'd fallen face-first into the pond and was just lying there, her nightgown spread out around her." He took a shaky breath. "I pulled her out and turned her over. She was alive, but only just. I gave her some CPR, which I know how to do from my army days, and she coughed and brought up all the water she'd swallowed. I took her up to bed and called the ambulance."

He glanced at his wife. "It was a very close call."

Violeta nodded sagely. "The ambulance came and took her into hospital for the night. The next day she was back, a little pale, but she didn't mention the incident, and we never spoke of it again."

"How strange," murmured Daisy. "You mean she didn't even say thank you?"

Violeta looked at Pepe and gave a little nod.

"A few weeks ago a journalist came sniffing around. Serena refused to see him, so he tried his luck with us. He asked why Serena had been hospitalized. We declined to comment and he went on his way." Pepe took a shaky breath. "A few days later Serena deposited a large amount of money into my bank account."

"She was trying to buy our silence," said Violeta. "But we'd never have told anyone anyway."

"How much?" Paul stared at Pepe.

"A hundred thousand pounds." The groundsman met the inspector's gaze. "That's what we were discussing on the lawn that day. I told her I didn't want her money, I would have done the same for anyone, but she insisted. She got quite angry when I said we'd transfer it back to her."

"And did you?" asked Daisy, glancing from one to the other.

"I'm ashamed to say we didn't," said Pepe.

Violeta shrugged. "Serena wouldn't hear of it, and Pepe has such bad rheumatism in his hands, we decided to use the money so he could have an operation."

"That makes sense." Serena didn't need the money—not then, and definitely not now.

"So, do you think Serena tried to commit suicide?" Paul asked the question they'd all been thinking.

Pepe's shoulders sagged. "I don't know. It could have been an accident. She was very drunk."

But Violeta scoffed. "The drinking was not uncommon; however, she'd never really been one for pills before. The drink usually knocked her right out."

"So she *was* trying to kill herself," Daisy surmised.

Violeta's voice dropped to a whisper. "Well, she was certainly unhappy enough to try."

Chapter Nineteen

Floria stood up and banged a teaspoon against her champagne glass. The noise quietened down. She thanked the guests for coming and said a few words about Serena. Floria was great at impromptu speeches—better than planned ones, in fact—and Daisy was surprised to hear her tell a story of how as a girl, she used to sneak out of her room and watch from the landing as the glamorous guests danced and cavorted below. She made her mother's life seem like a fairy tale, while Daisy knew it had been anything but, particularly for those closest to her. Then Floria gave a toast, and everyone clapped.

Sir Ranulph sipped a cup of tea, a faraway look in his eyes. "How are you holding up?" Daisy sat down next to him.

"That was a lovely speech Floria made," he said gruffly. "Serena didn't deserve a daughter like her."

Daisy patted his hand. "Floria's been marvelous. She's organized everything perfectly, and I've never seen Brompton Court looking so tidy."

Sir Ranulph grunted. "We're inundated with guests staying the night. Did Floria tell you? She's had the cleaners in for two days. No wonder the place is spotless. Serena was never much of a housekeeper, and poor Violeta couldn't cope with more than a few rooms."

Daisy chuckled at the thought of Serena playing housekeeper. "Congratulations, by the way. I heard Brompton Court is yours. Will you move back now?"

The old man nodded. "I didn't expect Serena to be so generous. I felt sure Collin was going to get the house, which would have been a tragedy."

"Perhaps she knew how much you loved it," said Daisy with a smile.

Sir Ranulph pursed his lips. "I didn't think she had it in her. Also, what she did for her daughters and the housekeeper. What a surprise."

"Human nature can surprise one." Daisy reached for a mini sausage roll from the tray of a passing waiter. Perhaps Serena had gone soft in her old age. Still, it didn't clarify who she was going to cut out of the will. Could it have been Ranulph? Perhaps she'd felt he didn't deserve Brompton Court after all. Was that the favor she'd been talking about? She studied the frail old man. He was rich in his own right. He'd made a mint managing Serena in the years they'd been together, and after that he'd gone on to manage several other classical music starlets. He didn't need Brompton Court. He had a lovely villa in the south of France. She'd been there with Floria on several occasions. It wasn't as large or majestic as Brompton Court, but it had a faded grandeur that was charming and, of course, it was also worth a fortune. No, Sir Ranulph didn't have a motive, not to mention the fact that he hadn't been in the country at the time of the murder.

"It's rather hot in here." Sir Ranulph attempted to get

to his feet. Daisy helped him up. "I think I'll go for a little stroll out in the garden."

Floria was on her way over to talk to Daisy when she got waylaid by Collin, buoyed up with scotch. "Floria, darling, you'll never guess who I saw at Marseilles airport," he said in a booming voice.

Sir Ranulph stumbled, and Floria, ignoring Collin, rushed to help him. "Dad, are you okay? Perhaps we'd better get you lying down."

"Yes," he nodded, clutching his cane. "That might be a good idea. It's been a very stressful day."

"Who did you see, Collin?" asked Daisy, but he was staring at Penny, who was laughing at something Niall had said.

"Oh, nothing. Never mind. I need a refill." He turned and left the room, no doubt headed back to the library and his private stash of Johnnie Walker Black Label.

Paul brought Daisy a much-needed drink. "I can't get my head around this case," he admitted, rubbing his eyes. She was reminded of how little sleep he'd had since it began. "There were no fingerprints other than Collin's found on the painting, so whoever stole it—or pretended to steal it—wore gloves. Then there's what Hubert said about it being a fake. Now that's interesting, and I can't help thinking there might be something in it. I think I'll go have a word with him. Have you seen him anywhere?"

Daisy shook her head. "I haven't seen him since the argument with Collin. Have you tried outside, in the garden? He did say he was going to get some air."

Floria, who'd seen to her father, returned with the bespectacled Kurt Bachmann in tow. He'd already spoken to Mimi and Donna, and had given them as much information as he could about their birth. The doctor was saying, "I remember seeing your mother perform in Milan; it must have been in the summer of '92. My word, she was amazing."

"The summer of 1992." Floria frowned. "Are you sure? I was born in August of 1992, so she would have been heavily pregnant with me at that point."

"Well, if she was, she carried it very well. I don't remember her being pregnant, but I could have been mistaken." He smiled at her. "Maybe it was a different year. My memory isn't what it used to be. You must be very proud of your mother, dear. What a shame she stopped performing, and now, with her passing, the world has lost an incredible talent." He shook his head at the travesty of it all.

Floria grimaced. "Well, thank you for coming to the reception, Dr. Bachmann. I'm sure Mimi and Donna are very grateful."

He smiled benevolently. "I hope I have managed to fill in some of the gaps in their past. It's so important to know one's roots, don't you think?"

Floria was about to walk him outside to the waiting taxi when an extremely flushed Penny rushed in, looking wildly around her. She grabbed Floria's arm. "Oh my God! You must call an ambulance. Something terrible has happened."

"What is it?"

"It's Mr. Harrison. We've just found his body in the rose garden."

Chapter Twenty

Everybody rushed to the door, but DI McGuinness stood there with his hands up. "Hold it," he bellowed.

Everybody stopped.

"Nobody is going outside until I say so. I'm afraid until I've investigated what's happened, no one is to leave. You will all remain indoors, preferably in the parlor, until I get back. Is that understood?"

"But I was about to leave," spluttered Carmen, who'd been tied up with Greg and the legalities of inheriting millions of pounds. The solicitor wanted to get her to sign the documents before she flew back to Barcelona.

"I said nobody." His tone didn't leave much room for disagreement. "Greg, see to it that no one leaves."

Greg nodded and, giving Carmen a sympathetic smile, set about shepherding everyone back into the parlor.

Paul turned to Dr. Bachmann. "Doctor, if you wouldn't mind coming with us?"

Then, with Daisy and Floria on his heels and the elderly gynecologist bringing up the rear, Paul marched outside and around the house to the rose garden. Niall stood beside the prostrate figure of Collin, guarding the body.

"I think he's been stabbed," he said, as somber as Daisy had ever seen him.

Paul bent down to take a closer look, but was careful not to touch the body. "Doctor, could you confirm?"

Dr. Bachmann knelt down beside him and very gently reached over the body to feel for a pulse. After a long moment he looked up and shook his head. "I'm afraid not."

Paul sighed and turned to Niall. "How did you come to discover him?"

"Penny and I were taking a stroll. We decided to take a look at the rose garden, and that's when we found him. He was just lying here, dead, behind the Lady of Shallots."

"You know your roses." Paul stood up, his eyes still on the body. "Judging from the blood underneath his stomach, I'd agree with your assumption, but I can't turn him over until the medical examiner gets here. Doctor, what is your opinion?"

Dr. Bachman got to his feet by way of his knees and inspected the body from the other side. "I agree. Abdominal wound. He probably bled out in a few minutes."

Daisy cringed. How awful. To think they'd been speaking to him in the library only a short time ago. How could this have happened so quickly?

"Did you see anyone lurking around when you were taking your walk?" Daisy asked Niall.

He shook his head. "No, we didn't see a soul once we'd rounded the corner of the house. There were a few people smoking outside the front entrance, but that's about it."

Paul nodded. "Thank you, Doctor; you can return to the house. Mr. Barclay, if you don't mind making sure everyone stays out of the rose garden while I make a few phone calls? This area must be kept clear." Niall nodded, and Paul strode off to call it in.

"How could this happen?" Floria asked as they moved away from Collin's body. She'd turned as pale as the cream Desdemona behind her and was trembling uncontrollably. Daisy wrapped an arm around her shaking shoulders. "Let's go inside. I think we all need a stiff drink. Doctor, will you accompany us?"

"Of course." The old man looked quite shaken. Daisy felt sorry for him. He'd been so excited to meet Serena's offspring, the children he'd delivered almost three decades ago, and now this . . .

Her own nerves were frayed. Was this the same person who'd murdered Serena? Was he or she lurking in their midst? Had the killer been at the reception this whole time? She shivered, despite the warm afternoon.

A short time later, sirens could be heard coming up the drive.

"I feel like a prisoner," huffed Hubert while the guests waited for DI McGuinness to get back and tell them when they could go home. The detective inspector was still at the crime scene with the medical examiner and forensic team.

"You were the one fighting with him earlier," said a short man with thinning hair. Daisy thought he might be a music producer.

"What are you implying? That I killed him?" Hubert stood up and glared at the man, who just shrugged. Nobody said anything. Hubert glanced around the room, then sank into a chair. "I suppose that's what you all think?"

The silence was damning.

"Let's not jump to any conclusions," said Greg, still in charge. The last thing they needed was everyone turning on poor Hubert. But tensions were high. There was a killer in their midst and everyone was on edge.

Mimi and Donna sat huddled together, while Carmen tapped away furiously on her phone. Daisy tried to think, which wasn't easy when her head was spinning. Where had everyone been when Collin had been killed? It must have happened in the last hour—no, it hadn't even been that long—the last twenty minutes, which meant Sir Ranulph had been upstairs resting, Niall had been strolling in the garden with Penny, and Hubert had presumably been here.

"Did you see Hubert come in?" Daisy whispered to Greg, who shook his head.

"No, sorry. I can't say I noticed."

She asked Floria, Mimi and Donna the same thing. They all remembered seeing him storm out after the argument, but none of them could recall seeing him come back in. She sidled over to Hubert, who was sitting with his head in his hands, a stiff drink on the windowsill behind him. "I'm sorry, Hubert, but I have to ask. How long were you outside after the fight?"

He stared at her and said miserably, "'Et tu, Brute?'"

Daisy whispered urgently, "Listen to me. If you can prove you were inside the house, you'd have an alibi; then you'd be in the clear."

His face lit up. "Yes, I was here. I was only out there for a few minutes, but it was too warm, so I came back inside. I went to the loo and then to the kitchen to pour myself a glass of Serena's vintage red that she keeps in the pantry. I was on my way back when that girl ran in saying Collin was dead."

Daisy's heart sank. "Did anyone see you? Not in the loo, I mean, but on the way there or back, or in the kitchen? Was Violeta there?"

His face fell. "No, there was nobody in the kitchen, and I went to the upstairs loo; it's much more private than the downstairs one."

Daisy sighed. She feared Hubert was going to have a hard time proving his innocence. Everyone saw him go outside, where he could have lingered until Collin came out, murdered him, then snuck back into the house and carried on as normal. No one would have been the wiser. Which begged the question, did he kill Serena too?

Greg beckoned from across the room.

"I need to tell you something in private," he whispered. They went into the hallway and stood to the side of the grand staircase, where it was darker and more secluded. "It's about Hubert. He's declared bankruptcy."

"What?" Daisy stared at him. "You mean he's broke?"

"Absolutely," Greg confirmed. "He filed with my firm last week. Hasn't got two pennies to rub together."

"But what about the antique store?"

"They can't cover their overheads. We're going to sell off the stock and shut down the business."

Daisy grimaced. "This is not looking good for Hubert."

Sir Ranulph appeared on the landing. "What's all the furor? Daisy, where is Floria?"

"I'll just get her for you, Sir Ranulph."

Floria went upstairs to tend to her father, leaving Mimi and Donna looking stunned in the lounge. They'd decided not to wait with the rest of the guests in the parlor, preferring a little privacy.

DI McGuinness popped his head around the door. "Daisy, have you got a moment?"

Daisy went to join him. "What have you discovered?"

"Stab wound to the abdomen. The doctor says he would have died within minutes, so that puts time of death at about quarter past five."

"How awful. Poor Collin."

"There's no sign of the murder weapon."

"So, we're looking for a knife?"

"Yes. The search team has just arrived with a warrant. I'm going to need all of you to move into the parlor as well, while they search the premises. I'm afraid it could take a while."

"Do you need any help?"

He shook his head. "No, we have it under control. Perhaps you can do what you do best and question the guests. Maybe someone saw something."

"I'll try, but so far it looks like everyone thinks Hubert did it."

"That's certainly a consideration. Make sure he's in the parlor at all times. I don't want him making a run for it."

"Okay, sure." Somehow she couldn't picture Hubert as a knife-wielding murderer. It was totally incongruous to everything she knew about him, and the evidence at this stage was purely circumstantial. Yes, he'd had a fight with Collin before the murder, but perhaps the killer had used that to his advantage. It was a devious trick, especially because Hubert had gone outside to get some air twenty minutes before Collin's body had been discovered. A little too contrived for her liking.

Daisy ushered Mimi and Donna into the parlor, which was uncomfortably hot with so many bodies in it. Floria was still upstairs with her father. The windows were open fully, but it didn't help much. Carmen stood by herself with her earphones in and ignored everyone, while Daisy apologized and reassured the guests that they'd be allowed to go home soon. Mimi and Donna appeared a little shell-shocked but stood quietly together and didn't make a fuss. Greg took his job as doorman very seriously and wouldn't let anyone out, not even for a toilet break. He also kept a sharp eye on Hubert, who sat in the corner sipping his whiskey, a thoroughly defeated expression on his face.

It was only when Daisy, who went to stand by the window, saw Paul usher in the forensic search team, that she remembered she'd forgotten to tell him about the bankruptcy.

Chapter Twenty-One

"Father's not doing too well," Floria told Daisy when she'd returned to the parlor. "His pulse is all over the place and he's sweating up a storm. It must be the shock."

"I'll go to see him," said Daisy. "Perhaps you can make him a cold beverage?"

Greg let them out, much to the annoyance of the other guests. Daisy went upstairs to the guest bedroom where Sir Ranulph was resting. He really didn't look well. His skin was tinged with gray and his shirt was damp with perspiration.

"I'll get you a cool cloth."

She went to get a flannel from the en suite bathroom. Returning, she placed it on his forehead. "There you go, that should help a bit."

"Is Collin really dead?" His voice was raspy.

"I'm afraid so, but you mustn't concern yourself. The police are here and they've got everything under control."

He nodded and lay his head back on the pillows. Floria came in with a jug of iced water. "Here, Dad, have some of this."

She poured him a glass and held it to his mouth as he

drank, after which he lay his head back down and closed his eyes. "Thank you, my darling Floria. What would I do without you?"

Floria sat down on the bed beside him, knocking over his cane. Daisy picked it up and leaned it against the bed-side table.

"Sorry, damn thing's always getting in the way," murmured Sir Ranulph.

"I'll stay with him a bit," said Floria. "Let me know if anything else happens downstairs."

Daisy nodded at her friend and left the room. Something was bothering her, but she couldn't put her finger on it. Perhaps it was a number of things, like little pieces of a puzzle all floating around in front of her eyes, waiting to be slotted into place. She frowned and sat down at the top of the stairs under the portrait of Serena. There was a lot of activity in the house. The forensic search team, dressed head-to-toe in white overalls, methodically searched every room. Soon they'd go upstairs. Would they find the murder weapon? It had to be here somewhere. Whoever had killed Collin had a very short space of time in which to do it, so they'd either still have the knife on them or they'd hidden it somewhere between the rose garden and the house.

Two police officers, one male and one female, were now in the parlor. Greg beckoned for her to join them. The guests were being searched. The men had to form one line and the women another.

"This is an outrage," huffed a ravishing Indian lady in a sari who Daisy knew to be a friend of Serena's. She was patted down by the female officer, then asked to empty out her handbag.

Hubert was searched along with everyone else, but the knife didn't turn up. Daisy studied the faces of the guests to see if anyone appeared nervous, but nobody stood out. She too was searched, as was Greg and Violeta and Pepe, who had been called in from the cottage. The search turned up two spliffs and a gram of cocaine, which were immediately confiscated, but no murder weapon.

They shunted everybody into the living room in order to search the parlor, after which they moved upstairs. They'd only been up there for ten minutes when a cry rang out. "Got something!"

Daisy poked her head out of the living room. "What have they found?"

"I think it's the knife," whispered Greg who, as guardsman, was standing just outside the door.

"Where?" hissed back Daisy.

He shrugged. "I don't know yet. Somewhere in the west wing."

DI McGuinness, his sergeant, Buckley, and a handful of uniformed coppers met in the parlor. They shut the door so no one else could overhear them. Then the door opened and two police officers emerged, serious expressions on their faces. They nodded to Greg to stand back, and then entered the living room, where all the guests were gathered.

"Mr. Hubert Laughton?" said one of them.

Hubert stood up. "That's me."

"We're arresting you for the murder of Collin Harrison. You have the right to remain silent." The rest of the guests stared in horror as the policeman read Hubert his rights.

"Excuse me, but why are you arresting this man?"

asked Greg, going into solicitor mode. "What evidence do you have?"

"The murder weapon was found in his jacket pocket," explained one of the officers. "Is that evidence enough for you?"

"In *my* jacket pocket?" repeated Hubert, who'd gone deathly pale. "I don't even know where my jacket is."

"It was in the upstairs bathroom. Come on, please. We have to take you in now."

Daisy followed Hubert as the policemen led him out of the house and into a waiting police car. The guests had fallen into a shocked silence.

"Was the knife really found in his pocket?" Daisy asked Paul as the police car drove away.

"I'm afraid so." He gave Daisy a pointed look. "And I know you're going to say anyone could have planted it there, which is true, but we have to act on the evidence."

"Something's not right." Daisy frowned. "I know Hubert was bankrupt, but I don't think he's a killer. The psychology is all wrong."

"He's bankrupt?"

"Oh, yes. I forgot to tell you. Greg said he filed with his company last week."

Paul grimaced. "That's not going to look good in court. The prosecution will argue he was desperate and so attempted to steal the painting to sell it on the black market. He'd have the contacts to do that."

"Yes, but the painting wasn't stolen. It was hidden. Why would the thief do that?"

"To come back and get it at a later stage. Perhaps he didn't want to be caught with it? I don't know, but to be honest, it doesn't matter what I think. It will be up to the jury at the trial."

Daisy shook her head. "Why kill Collin? What motive could Hubert possibly have?"

"You saw the fight earlier. Perhaps Hubert was getting his revenge. Collin did very nearly throttle him."

"Hubert isn't a violent man. I'm sorry, Paul. I just don't see it. If that painting is a fake—and that's a big if—it would give Collin motive to kill Hubert, not the other way around. Collin wouldn't want to risk exposure."

"Perhaps Collin did threaten him and Hubert reacted in self-defense."

Daisy thought about that for a moment. "That would make more sense, but Hubert didn't look like he'd just killed someone. There was no blood on his hands or shirt-sleeves, he wasn't sweating and didn't appear nervous. In fact, he was as surprised as everyone else when the police arrested him."

Paul sighed. "Daisy, I know you're trying to help, but the evidence is indisputable. Until we can prove other-wise, the murder weapon was found in his jacket pocket in the bathroom that he admits he went to. It doesn't really get any clearer than that."

Daisy snorted. "That's what I'm afraid of."

She stalked back into the house. The guests were being allowed to leave now, and a steady stream of black taxi-cabs had begun to pull up outside the mansion.

"It's about bloody time," grumbled Colonel Snodgrass. "My hip is playing up something terrible."

"I'd better call Lucian," said Floria dismally. She looked shattered. "He'll be devastated to hear about Hubert. I can't believe he murdered Mother and Collin."

Daisy didn't know what to say. She kept picturing Hubert's face as he was arrested. Incomprehension, disbelief, confusion.

The man had been totally bewildered by what was happening. That wasn't the face of a guilty person. No, she was very much afraid Hubert had been set up, and very cleverly so. The evidence was indisputable, as Paul had said. The murder weapon found in his jacket pocket. That made all the other circumstantial evidence fall into place. Poor Hubert wouldn't stand a chance in court.

She sighed and shook her head, feeling the effects of the day weighing down on her too.

"I can't believe it either."

Chapter Twenty-Two

The heat from the sun was already intense when Daisy opened the salon at eight a.m. the following morning. Walking the short distance from her home to Ooh La La had made her perspire. It was going to be another scorching day. The telephone was ringing as she rushed inside. Monday was usually a quiet day, but it seemed everyone wanted to find out what had happened at Brompton Court last night. News of Hubert's arrest had spread around the village like wildfire, and every available slot in Daisy's schedule was filled by nine thirty.

"That's it. We're fully booked for today. I can't squeeze anyone else in," she told Penny as she penciled a new customer into her lunch hour.

"Murder is great for business," said Krish, comb behind his ear, his fingers tapping away on his iPhone. "And my social life. I've been inundated with invitations to all the hottest parties in London."

Asa wagged her finger at him. "You were Instagramming up a storm yesterday, you naughty boy."

He grinned. "I'm in talks with *The Star* for an exclusive. The inside scoop on the murder at Brompton Court."

Daisy shook her head. "You are a PR nightmare. I'm sure DI McGuinness wouldn't want you divulging details of the case to the press."

He had the grace to look offended. "Scandal is a lucrative business. They're offering a fortune for my story. How can I refuse? It's going to come out anyway, I'm just helping them get the facts straight." He gave a little pout. "I promise I won't say anything to upset your Mr. McGuinness."

"Hmm . . . " Daisy supposed he was right. The story was already out there, and with all those publicity-hungry guests at the reception, it wouldn't be long before it was in every tabloid and magazine in the country.

Poor Floria. She didn't need this. Not after the emotion of the funeral and meeting her sisters for the first time. At least they were all in it together. If nothing else, they would know one another fairly well by the end of it. There was nothing like a double murder to break the ice.

"I heard Hubert accused Collin of faking the Modigliani," said Mrs. Jenkins, who'd caught the bus from the senior living community on the outskirts of the village to come in for her nine o'clock. How she'd come across that little nugget, Daisy had no idea. "Is it true? I studied art in Florence as a girl."

Daisy smiled at the old lady who, despite her advanced years, was as sharp as a pair of scissors. "Yes, he did accuse it of being a fake, but that hasn't been proven. The police are still looking into it."

She scoffed. "What do they know? Modigliani was copied many times. There are reputedly hundreds of forgeries out there. Why, only last year an exhibition in Zürich had to be closed down because the reclining nude was a fake. If the professionals didn't notice, your police squad aren't going to be of much use."

She had a point, although Daisy liked to think the art fraud department knew what they were doing. "I'm sure they work with experts, Mrs. Jenkins. Art fraud is a very specialized field, as you know. Besides, Collin had the provenance in his study, I saw it with my own eyes."

The old lady pursed her lips. "And provenances can't be forged?" She smiled at Daisy like one would an errant child. "Anyway, dear, I'm sure Mr. Harrison bought it in good faith. He's a dealer, after all. If it is a fake, it's likely he didn't know." She paused to study herself in the mirror. "I'd like the usual, please, dear."

Daisy got to work, but Mrs. Jenkins wasn't finished. "That Hubert Laughton," she said while Daisy was setting her hair. "He's the real deal. I saw him on *Antiques Road-show* a couple of years ago, and trust me, he knows his stuff. If he suspects the painting is a fake, I'd tend to believe him."

Daisy had just put Mrs. Jenkins under the dryer when a thought hit her. She riffled through her handbag for the scrunched-up ball of paper containing the telephone number of the art store in Paris, the one she'd found in Collin's wastepaper basket. It was in here somewhere.

"Got it!" She pulled it out triumphantly, then went to talk to Krish. He stopped what he was doing.

"I need you to contact your friend in Paris, the one who works at the Louvre. Could you get him to go to an art store for me? Here's what I want him to say . . . "

* * *

DI McGuinness was pulling down the photographs from the whiteboard in the Scout hall and placing them in a cardboard box when Daisy arrived.

"Packing up?"

The garage door was wide open, letting in as much fresh air as possible, but it was still stiflingly hot inside. The corrugated iron roof retained the heat like a sauna.

"Unfortunately, yes." He smiled at her. "Case closed, I'm afraid. We're going to prosecute."

Daisy nodded. "Did Hubert confess?"

Paul gave her an odd look. "No, of course not. He still maintains his innocence. He said he saw something in the painting that made him doubt its authenticity and confronted Collin about it. That's the last contact he had with the victim." He sighed. "Unfortunately, the evidence says otherwise."

"Do *you* believe he's guilty?"

Paul shrugged. "It doesn't matter what I believe. My job is to gather the evidence, not make a judgment. The prosecution has enough to take it to court, so that's the process we have to follow."

Daisy looked around her. The nature posters on the walls had been updated and now included ones on survival tactics, first aid and effective communication techniques, but the hall looked and smelled just like it had when she'd been a member. Memories of her time in the Girl Guides flooded back: being awarded her badges at the front of the hall, learning survival skills and laughing and joking with the other girls, most of whom were married with children now.

"What are you doing here?" Paul took down the last

suspect photograph and turned to face her. "Did you come to say goodbye?"

Daisy smiled. "Actually, I want to ask you to look up something for me, if it's not too late."

"Well, the case is closed, but I might be able to pull a few strings. What is it you want me to check?"

She told him what it was.

He pursed his lips and gave a low whistle. "You really think that's possible?"

She shrugged. "I don't know, but I think we ought to check before we send Hubert to the gallows. It's something Collin said before he died. It's been bothering me ever since."

"Fair enough. I'll look into it and get back to you."

Daisy nodded. "Thanks, Paul."

It had been fun working with him; she'd enjoyed analyzing suspects and discussing the case, more so than she cared to admit. But how to tell someone that without sounding sappy?

"No problem."

He hesitated, like he was about to say something else, but then decided against it. Perhaps he'd had the same inclination as her. Instead, he picked up the box. "That's the last of it."

The moment passed.

Daisy said goodbye and took off across the meadow toward her house. Behind her, she heard Paul pull down the noisy garage door and lock it, before getting into his car and driving away.

Chapter Twenty-Three

"What's going on?" inquired Floria as Daisy walked into Brompton Court followed by DI McGuinness and Sergeant Buckley. "Carmen's just arrived in a cab and is in a foul mood."

A uniformed police officer remained at the front door, and there was another outside in the police car that had followed Paul and Daisy to the premises.

Greg had also been summoned, but he didn't know why. On seeing the police presence, he frowned. He was smart enough to know something was going down. "I have work to do, Detective Inspector," he said irritably.

"This won't take long." Paul turned to Floria. "Can we get your father downstairs, as well as Violeta and Pepe? I have an announcement to make."

"Of course." Floria left to do as requested, shooting a worried look in Daisy's direction. A short time later the entire household, including Carmen, Mimi and Donna, were assembled in the parlor. The furniture had reverted back to normal after the reception and someone had even found time to vacuum the carpet. There wasn't a crumb in sight.

"What's the meaning of this?" Sir Ranulph tapped his cane on the floor. "I'm not well, you know."

"It'll all become clear in a moment." Paul studied them each in turn. "I'm sorry to disrupt your day, but some new evidence has come to light that we thought pertinent to share with you."

"What new evidence?" asked Floria, signs of emotional upheaval evident in her face. Dark shadows framed her normally sparkling eyes, and her skin looked tired and sallow. Daisy's heart went out to her.

"This case has been a riddle from the start," Paul began. "First, we thought it was Sergio, Tatiana's boyfriend, who murdered Serena. The most obvious scenario was that he let himself in with Tatiana's key with the purpose of stealing the painting, but then Serena woke up and caught him in the act. In a panic, he hit her on the head and pushed her over the balustrade to her death. We've since discovered this wasn't the case."

"But he did break in," whispered Violeta.

"Oh yes, he did. He admitted as much, but then he saw Serena lying at the foot of the stairs and panicked. He decided the best thing to do was to get the hell out and pretend he'd never been here at all. So he carefully locked the front door and ran away. Indeed, the evidence—or rather, lack thereof—seems to support this."

Eight pale faces, excluding Daisy's, whose was rather flushed, stared back at him.

"We realized that whoever had committed the murder must have had intimate knowledge of the mansion. They knew where the priest hole was, for example, and they must have had a key to the premises."

"I hope you're not suggesting we had anything to do

with it," gasped Violeta. Her husband laid a calming hand on her shoulder.

"No, of course not," said Daisy hurriedly.

"Even though you did have motive," interjected Paul. "Your husband needs an operation, so you needed money."

"But . . . " interrupted Pepe.

Paul held up a hand. "I know Serena paid you off for keeping quiet about her suicide attempt, which means you didn't have to steal the painting."

"Suicide attempt?" Floria mumbled, uncomprehending. "What suicide attempt?" She glanced at Daisy and then the inspector. "I don't understand . . .?"

"We wouldn't have resorted to theft anyway." Violeta looked horrified. "What kind of people do you think we are?"

"It was a logical thought process, Violeta," explained Daisy. "He meant no harm by it."

Violeta nodded, although the consternation hadn't left her face.

"What suicide attempt?" Floria said, louder this time. There was a hysterical edge to her voice. "Will someone please tell me what's going on?"

Violeta wrung her hands. "Serena overdosed on sleeping pills about a month ago. Pepe found her lying in the fountain. She would have drowned if he hadn't saved her."

Floria spun around. "Is it true, Pepe? You saved her life?"

He nodded sadly. "Not that it did much good."

Floria put her hand over her mouth. "I had no idea." She sunk down on a wooden-backed chair that stood against the wall. "Why didn't someone tell me?"

"We didn't want to worry you," whispered Violeta. "And Serena swore us to secrecy."

Paul didn't want to lose his train of thought. "Then there was you, Carmen."

Carmen glanced up from her position on the chaise longue. *"Qué?"*

"You lied to us," said Daisy softly. "You said you flew over to London the day before the funeral when, in fact, you flew in a week ago."

Donna gasped, while Mimi glared at Carmen. "You just can't help yourself, can you? Looking down your nose at everyone when in fact you've been lying through your teeth."

Carmen's features tightened, and she looked like she was about to pounce.

"You had ample motive," added Daisy quickly, bringing the attention back to her. "God knows you felt abandoned by Serena. She left you when you were a baby and handed you over to your father to raise. She refused to support you, to have anything to do with you."

Anger flashed across Carmen's face. "She left me to grow up in poverty when she had so much money she didn't know what to do with it all."

"I'm sorry you had such a hard time growing up," said Daisy, feeling pity for the girl.

Carmen scowled. "It's none of your business."

"But it is our business," cut in Floria. "You are part of this family now, whether you like it or not. Don't you see, Serena abandoned us all."

Carmen scoffed. "She didn't abandon you. Look at this place. You have everything you want."

"Yes, she did," Floria got to her feet. "She palmed me

off on nannies and au pairs from the moment I was born. I never saw her. She didn't speak to me. In fact, I had no idea who she really was. My parents traveled constantly; they were always on tour. Then, when I was eleven, she sent me off to boarding school in another county forty miles away, and it was full-time boarding, so I wasn't even allowed home on weekends."

"It's true," sniffed Violeta. "I felt so sorry for you, poor lamb. Every holiday you floated around this place by yourself, and when your mother was home she'd screech at you for getting underfoot."

"I didn't have it any better than you." Floria fought back tears. "True, I had money, but no love, no affection. I may as well have been part of the furniture."

"Oh, Floria." Sir Ranulph made a strangling noise. "I'm so sorry you had to go through all that. I should have realized. Your mother was a selfish woman; she cared about nothing other than her singing and I . . . well, I suppose I was so caught up in her career that I didn't think about anything else."

"I know, Dad." Floria sat down again, and Mimi gripped her hand.

"Can I just get this straight?" Greg turned to Carmen. "When I called to tell you Serena had died—you were actually in London?"

Carmen looked shifty.

"But why? Why were you here?"

Carmen glanced at Paul. "You can tell them," he said.

"If you must know, I was spying on my boyfriend. There, I've said it. Is everybody happy now?" Her eyes blazed as she admitted it. "I followed him to London because I suspected he was having an affair."

"Your boyfriend?" Floria stared at her.

"Yes, that is why I was here. I surprised him at the Hilton in Park Lane and we spent the week together."

"So, he wasn't cheating on you?" The question came from Mimi.

Carmen focused her fiery gaze on her. "No."

"That's why she was so hard to track down," said Daisy. "She wasn't in Spain at all. When she finally got Greg's message she lied and said she'd catch a flight to London as soon as possible."

"But why lie?" said Donna. "Why not just say you were already here."

"I saw the papers," she said sulkily. "I knew how it would look. I thought it would be better to pretend I was coming from Spain."

"It certainly complicated matters," said Paul. "You had ample motive, you hated your mother and you were in the country at the time. You could have come around to the house that Saturday night, and Serena, recognizing you, would have let you in. Then, it would have been simple to hit her on the head and throw her over the landing."

"It wasn't me," spat Carmen.

"What about the painting?" Floria pointed out.

"Ah, that is why this theory doesn't hold water." Paul tilted his head to the side. "Carmen couldn't possibly have known that there was a valuable painting upstairs, or in fact that there were any valuables in the house. And she certainly wouldn't have been aware of the priest hole in the pantry. Besides, the receptionist at the Hilton corroborated your alibi."

"See." Carmen sat back and folded her arms across her chest. "It wasn't me."

"No," said Paul. "It wasn't you. It was someone who knew the house intimately, who had a key to the front door, who knew Serena's habits and who had a strong motive for killing her."

His gaze shifted to Sir Ranulph.

"No way!" Floria jumped off the sofa. "You can't be suggesting it was Father."

"I think you'd better listen to what he has to say first, Floria," Daisy said softly.

Floria knelt by her father's side and took his hand in hers.

"Sir Ranulph, you had a key to the property that you claimed you'd lost many years ago. Well, I think you still have that key. You also knew about the priest hole in the pantry and the Modigliani upstairs in Collin's study. But robbery wasn't your motive, was it?"

Sir Ranulph didn't say anything. He just stared at Paul through rheumy eyes and waited for him to continue.

"You wanted to murder your ex-wife, Serena Levanté."

"No," Floria gasped. "It's not true. Tell them it's not true, Daddy."

Daisy felt her heart break for Floria. "It was you who Collin saw at the airport in Marseilles, wasn't it, Sir Ranulph? He'd just arrived to spend the weekend with his mistress in Lourmarin and you were leaving, on your way to London to kill Serena."

Floria stared at her in horror. "Daisy, you've got it all wrong."

But Sir Ranulph didn't deny it. He just sat there, staring into the distance, like he wasn't fully with it.

"I'm sorry Floria, but it's the truth. He murdered Serena,

but he did it to protect you. It was done out of love for you."

"I don't understand." Floria clutched her father's hand and stared up at his face.

Daisy perched on the coffee table in front of Floria, who was still kneeling on the floor. "Can I tell her, Sir Ranulph?"

The old man nodded, his lip quivering. A single tear ran down his cheek.

"Tell me what?" Floria was beside herself.

"That you are not Serena's biological daughter."

Gasps were heard around the room as what she said sank in.

"B–but Serena would have told me," stammered Greg. "I would have known."

"She was going to tell you, Greg," explained Daisy, turning to face him. "That's what she wanted to meet with you about, and that's the reason why she wanted to change her will."

"You mean she was going to cut Floria out of it?" whispered Donna, aghast.

Daisy looked at Sir Ranulph, who nodded sadly. "She phoned me the day before and told me what she planned to do." He gazed lovingly at Floria and stroked her hair. "I couldn't let her do that to you. Not after everything she'd put you through."

"No, Daddy. I don't believe you." Floria was crying now, the tears flowing freely down her cheeks.

"Floria was a baby when you met Serena, wasn't she?" Daisy asked Sir Ranulph.

He nodded wearily. He seemed to have aged consider-ably in the last few minutes. "Yes, your mother and I were very young when we had you. We weren't married, it was a mistake and she died in childbirth." His eyes glazed over as he remembered. "She was so beautiful, like an angel, with golden hair just like yours."

"I always wondered why I didn't take after Serena." Floria sniffed. "Look at all of you; you're all like her in some way. You've got dark hair, green eyes—her eyes—and her musical talent. I've got none of that."

Daisy put out a hand and touched her leg. "You've got plenty of other talents, Floria. Just because you're not like Serena doesn't make you any less worthy."

Paul added the final details. "So you caught a plane on Saturday evening to Gatwick, rented a car and drove to Brompton Court, where you used your key to get in. Serena heard you and woke up."

"She was drunk," said Sir Ranulph, a look of disgust on his face. "Drunker than I'd ever seen her. She could hardly walk straight. I hit her on the head with my cane and she collapsed on the landing, but she wasn't dead, only stunned. I knew that I had to kill her, but I didn't have the strength to hit her again, so I helped her up, then pushed her over the balustrade."

Floria cried out, then covered her mouth with her hands. The others stared at him in horror.

Sir Ranulph continued, oblivious to anyone else in the room. "It was surprisingly easy. She was so inebriated she fell over almost on her own accord."

"So that's why you got a new cane." Daisy nodded to the one positioned next to the armchair. "Your old one was the murder weapon."

Again he nodded.

"I threw it into the sea during the crossing back to France."

"You took the ferry to avoid the airports in case anyone was looking for you." Paul came a little closer. "Then, when Floria called you with the news about Serena's death, you caught another flight to London and arrived two days ago."

Floria stared at her father like she'd never seen him before. "You did all this to save me from being disinherited?"

He took her face in his hands. "I didn't know what to do. I tried reasoning with her, but she was adamant; you weren't her real daughter and she felt she didn't owe you anything. She could be so malicious, as you well know. I couldn't have her cutting you out of the will, not after everything you've done for her over the years. Even though she treated you appallingly, you put up with it all, helped organize her parties and soirées," he scoffed, "even her bloody funeral. She didn't deserve any of it. She didn't deserve you."

"Oh, Daddy." Floria flung herself into his arms. He held her like a child, before Paul gently pulled her away and passed her to Daisy.

"I'm afraid I'm going to have to arrest you now, Sir Ranulph."

The old man nodded and got unsteadily to his feet. "I understand. I'm ready."

"No," cried Floria, reaching for her father. Daisy held her tight while the other sisters looked on in shock. Even Carmen was silent.

Buckley came forward and led Sir Ranulph outside where the patrol car was waiting. At least they didn't put handcuffs on him. Daisy held on to Floria, who was verging on hysteria. As her father was put into the back of the vehicle, she made to go after him, but Daisy held her back. "No, Floria. You've got to let justice take its course. Your father knew what he was doing."

"But he did it for me," she sobbed, tears streaming down her face.

Daisy felt like crying herself.

"Yes," she whispered. "He did it for you."

Chapter Twenty-Four

After Sir Ranulph had been taken away in the squad car, Paul came back inside, his features taut. The emotion of the conviction had got to him too. Violeta had taken an inconsolable Floria up to her room and given her a mild sedative, but the rest of them were seated in the living room, still in shock after the morning's revelations.

"How did you work it out?" Greg asked Paul in awe.

Paul grinned and put a friendly arm around Daisy's shoulders. "Actually, it was Daisy who figured it out."

"I wish I'd been wrong." Daisy felt awful about causing Floria, her best friend, so much pain.

"It's not your fault," said Greg diplomatically. "Sir Ranulph was responsible for his own actions, and it seemed to me he knew exactly what he was doing."

"He planned it down to the last detail," said Paul. "He stole the Modigliani to make it look like a robbery, but he couldn't be seen with the painting, so he hid it in the priest hole instead, never dreaming that it would be found before he had a chance to come back for it."

"How on earth did you know Floria wasn't Serena's biological daughter?" Mimi asked Daisy, her legs curled underneath her on the couch. "I must admit I didn't see that one coming."

"Me neither." Donna shook her head.

"It was something that the Austrian doctor, Kurt Bachmann, said. He claimed he'd seen Serena live in Milan in '92, but that was the year Floria was born. Serena would have been pregnant with her at the time of the concert, but she wasn't. I Googled it last night. There's a photograph of Serena performing in Milan, and I can guarantee you she wasn't seven months pregnant. Not in that dress."

Mimi shook her head. "You're amazing, Daisy. You've got a real gift for this sort of thing."

"Keep on with that forensic psychology degree," chimed in Paul. "I think you're on the right track there."

"Did Sir Ranulph kill Collin too?" Greg poured himself a finger of scotch and offered the bottle around. Pepe accepted, but everyone else declined.

"Surely not," said Donna. "That was Hubert. We saw them arguing in the hall."

Daisy shook her head. "I'm afraid not, Donna. Collin spotted Sir Ranulph at the airport in Marseilles on his way here to murder Serena. He was about to say as much at the reception, but then Sir Ranulph stumbled and Floria rushed to help him, creating a diversion. After that, Collin thought he'd try to blackmail Sir Ranulph instead—he always was an opportunist—and they arranged to meet in the rose garden."

"But Sir Ranulph was in bed," said Donna, confused. "I saw Floria take him upstairs."

"He knows this house better than anyone," Daisy told her. "There's a staircase from the east wing, where the guest bedrooms are, which leads out into the garden. It would have taken no time at all for him to get to the rose garden that way without being seen. He met Collin, they argued and Sir Ranulph stabbed him in the stomach, leaving him to bleed to death."

"But the murder weapon was found in Hubert's jacket." Greg's eyes widened as realization dawned. "Oh, right. So Sir Ranulph planted it in the jacket because Hubert had left it in the upstairs loo."

"Conveniently," said Paul. "Sir Ranulph had to get rid of it, and who better to blame than the very man who Collin had had a public argument with earlier that evening."

"Clever," said Mimi with a shiver.

"I didn't think the old man had it in him," confessed Greg, shaking his head. "And all because he didn't want Floria to be disinherited."

"It's so sad," said Donna.

Carmen remained silent, but Mimi turned on her. "What do you think now, Carmen? Would you rather have had this fate? Look what Floria's going through. Serena let her down more than any of us. Perhaps you should think about that next time you turn up your nose at her."

"That's enough," said Donna with a rare show of fortitude. "I think we've all had more than enough trauma for one day."

At least Carmen had the grace to look ashamed.

"I think I'd better go." Daisy stood up. It had been an emotional morning and she didn't feel particularly happy about it. Yes, justice had been done, but it had destroyed Floria. Her mother not really her mother. Her father a murderer. The tabloids were going to have a field day with that one. She shook her head.

"You will look after Floria, won't you?" she said to Mimi and Donna. "She's going to need a lot of support right now."

"Of course," Donna replied, and Mimi nodded. "We'll make sure she's okay."

Daisy knew they would. The sisterly bond between them would grow stronger because of this, she had no doubt, and hopefully, in some small way, it would make Carmen realize she wasn't the only one who had suffered because of Serena's neglect. Perhaps something good would come out of this ghastly affair.

"I'll run you home," said Paul, putting an arm around her shoulders. She liked it. The weight of his arm comforted her and made her feel warm and appreciated.

She smiled up at him. "That would be great, thanks."

Greg made his excuses too. "I've got to get back to the office." He followed them out. "Sir Ranulph's conviction will cause complications with the execution of the will."

"You aren't going to cut Floria out?" asked Mimi, aghast.

"No, not unless you lot contest it."

They all shook their heads.

Greg smiled. "What I meant was, Brompton Court will go to Floria now."

"Well, that's something at least." Daisy was pleased. Floria deserved it.

Greg rolled his eyes. "I can't believe Serena's dead and buried and she's still my most difficult client."

Daisy's phone beeped as Paul turned out of Brompton Court's long, winding driveway and merged with the mainstream traffic.

"It's Krish." She opened the text message. "I asked him to check out that art shop in Paris that you called the other day."

"Why did you do that?" Paul glanced across at her. "I thought we wrote that off as one of Collin's random contacts."

"Let's just say I had a hunch." She read the message, then glanced up at Paul. "I was right! The art shop is a front for forged paintings."

"What?" He pulled over into a lay-by surrounded by trees. This section of the road cut through the woods, which covered most of the countryside between Brompton Court and Edgemead.

"Explain?"

"Okay. Krish got his friend who works at the Louvre to pay them a visit and commission a fake Modigliani. He told them their details had been passed on to him by a Mr. Collin Harrison."

Paul shook his head. "Sneaky."

Daisy grinned. "After some consideration they agreed to put him in touch with an artist who specializes in Modigliani. He's sent me the details."

Paul raised his eyebrows. "I'll pass them over to the relevant authorities. If what you're saying is true, Hubert may well have been right about that painting. It could have been a fake after all."

"Indeed. Poor Hubert; he's been through the ringer. I wonder how many of Collin's paintings have been forgeries? He may have built his entire business selling forged masterpieces. I always knew he had a dodgy past, but I didn't for a minute imagine he was tied up in art fraud."

"We'll let INTERPOL handle it. They have a division that specializes in international art fraud." He signaled and pulled off into the traffic.

"Are you going to take me home now?" Daisy asked. Part of her was emotionally drained, but another part wanted to drag out the drive as long as possible. Could it be she didn't want to say goodbye to Paul?

"I am." His eyes sparkled. "But only for a short while. I have to go back to the station to tie up the case, but how about we go to Nonna Lina's tonight? I'd like to have a decent conversation without having to dash off anywhere."

Daisy grinned. It seemed he'd solved the problem for her.

"Now that sounds like the perfect plan."

Don't miss the next delightful Daisy Thorne mystery

DEATH AT THE SALON

Coming soon from Kensington Publishing Corp.

Keep reading to enjoy the first chapter . . .

Chapter One

The tiny brass bell attached to the front door of Ooh La La hair salon tinkled as Liz Roberts, head of the Edgemead Women's Institute, marched in, bringing with her a blast of rain-drenched wind.

"Heavens, it's appalling out there," she said as she shook out her umbrella and left it dripping against the antique hatstand. "I trod in a puddle outside the Fox and Hound, and I swear I've ruined my new suede boots." She glanced disdainfully down at her feet.

"Can I take your coat?" Daisy smiled sympathetically.

Liz removed her practical Barbour raincoat and handed it over. "Thanks, Daisy dear. Oh, it is nice and warm in here. Hopefully, my shoes will dry out."

"Come on, we're over here." Daisy led her to one of the comfy leather chairs positioned in front of a gilt-framed mirror. "Would you like a cup of tea?"

"You wouldn't happen to have anything stronger, would you?" Liz arched an eyebrow. "I've had such a trying day."

Daisy hid her surprise. Liz seldom indulged. "Of course; you know me. I've always got a bottle of something in the back." She turned to Penny, who was sweeping up the hair from her last client. "Could you pour Liz a glass of the sav blanc?"

Liz picked up the latest edition of *Vogue* magazine and flicked through it without looking at any of the pages. "Thanks for fitting me in this late. I hope I'm not putting you out."

Daisy picked up her comb. The table containing the tint, foil wraps, and various utensils had been prepared in advance. Liz was having her usual mixture of highlights and lowlights. "We close at nine on Saturday, so you're our last customer of the day." It wasn't like she had anything better to do anyway, and the weather was so dire that the sofa, a takeaway pizza, and a boxed set was calling her name.

Penny returned with a glass of wine and handed it to Liz. "Thank you, dear."

Daisy noticed her hand was shaking. "Are you all right, Liz?"

The formidable face showed just a hint of vulnerability. "Yes, of course, dear. It's just that the speaker for this Thursday's meeting canceled at the last minute, leaving us in the lurch. She's pregnant." She rolled her eyes at Daisy. "Pregnant women are always so unreliable."

Liz Roberts wasn't known for her tact.

"What was she going to talk about?" Daisy asked.

"We were going to make Christmas wreaths." Her mouth turned down at the corners. "I have no idea what to do now. I suppose I'll have to ask Mrs. Radisson to give us her rosemary turkey stuffing demonstration again."

Daisy parted Liz's hair into segments and began to apply the tint. "I have a friend who makes her own Christmas cards. They're really lovely, with sparkles and little bows on them. If you want, I could ask her if she'd be prepared to do a workshop for you."

Liz's face lit up. "Oh, Daisy, would you? That would be fantastic. I really am at loose ends."

Daisy nodded. "No problem. I'll call her tonight."

Penny reappeared from the back wearing her coat and scarf. "Right. I'm off, Daisy. Thanks for letting me go early. I'll lock up next Saturday, I promise."

"That's okay. Have fun tonight at the hen party."

Penny glanced at her wristwatch. "I won't get there much before nine because I'm going home to change first. I'm meeting Niall later." Her eyes sparkled. Niall was Penny's new beau, and while Daisy didn't altogether approve of the match, she had to admit Penny seemed happy. Unfortunately, knowing Niall, the relationship was unlikely to last. Still, stranger things had happened.

"I'm sure the party will be going on for a while," said Daisy. "Those girls were gearing up for a big night." All three of Penny's model friends had been in earlier to get their hair done for tonight's celebrations. They'd bought a bottle of bubbly with them and were giggling merrily by the time they left.

Penny grinned. "Yes, they were. I'll see you on Monday. 'Bye."

After she left, Liz glanced up at Daisy. "That man is twice her age. He ought to be ashamed of himself."

Daisy shrugged. Niall was a notorious womanizer and an ex-husband of the late Dame Serena Levanté, the infamous opera diva who'd been murdered last year in her country mansion. It was Daisy who'd helped crack the case. "He is very handsome," she allowed.

Liz frowned. "If one goes in for that sort of thing. I'm more inclined to think it's his money she's after."

Daisy shook her head. "No, not Penny, she's not a gold digger." She wrapped a strip of foil around the highlight and squeezed it closed. "You have to admit, Niall does have something of the Heathcliff about him. I can picture him riding bareback through the moors on one of his prized racehorses, can't you?"

Liz gave her a sharp look. "Don't tell me you're smitten too?"

Daisy laughed. "You know me better than that, Liz. All I'm saying is that I can see the appeal."

Liz grunted.

Once the foils were done, Daisy placed Liz under the dryer and took the messy utensils and dishes into the kitchenette to wash up. BBC Radio 3 was playing *La Calisto*, Cavalli's opera of pursuit and transformation, and the dramatic music filled the salon. With a contented sigh, Daisy washed up and then poured herself a much-needed glass of wine. The back door was banging in the wind, so she wedged a piece of paper towel in the crack. Exactly ten minutes later she switched off the dryer.

"Come over to the basin," she told Liz, and proceeded to wash and condition her newly dyed hair.

"Do you want a trim?" Daisy asked once Liz was back in the chair in front of the mirror, admiring her new color.

"Yes, just half an inch off the bottom."

Daisy reached into the drawer for her scissors, but they weren't there. How strange. She always put them back in the top drawer of her workstation; in fact, she was fastidious about it. Her eyes roamed over the countertops, but they weren't there either. Frowning, she opened Penny's drawer and used hers. Each stylist had their own scissors to avoid confusion.

"How are things going with that hunky detective of yours, Daisy?" asked Liz, causing Daisy's head to pop up.

"I don't know what you mean," said Daisy, avoiding eye contact.

"I thought you two were a thing." Liz arched an over-plucked eyebrow.

Daisy took a gulp of her wine. "Oh, no. We worked together on that case last year, but that was it. There's nothing going on between us."

"If you say so, dear." Liz winked at her.

Daisy sighed. She hadn't seen Paul in months. He was situated in Guildford, which was a good forty-minute drive from Edgemead. He'd taken her out once after the Serena Levanté case, but then Daisy had gone away with her friend, Floria, to the south of France in the summer, and they'd lost touch after that. According to Krish, her senior stylist and an irrepressible gossip, Paul had been working on a high-profile case involving human traffickers and was making quite a name for himself.

"It's all thanks to you, Daisy," Krish had told her. "If you hadn't helped him crack the Levanté case, he'd still be doing the graveyard shift at the precinct."

She trimmed Liz's hair into a stylish bob, then blow-dried it. When she was done Liz was back to her perfectly coiffed self.

"Fabulous, thanks, dear," she said, admiring herself in the mirror. She smoothed a hand over her cheek, as if trying to iron out the wrinkles, and gave a little sigh. "I'm going to call an Uber because I don't want to ruin it the moment I walk outside. I'm meeting with the mayor tomorrow about the congestion between Esher and Edgemead. Did I tell you?"

"Yes, I think you did mention it," said Daisy. "And take your time; there's no rush."

Liz paid the bill, and once she'd gone, Daisy set about straightening up her salon. She liked this time of day, after the last customer had left, because time seemed to slow down. Cleaning while listening to music had become something of an evening ritual. It helped her unwind after the frenetic pace of the day and gave her a chance to recharge her batteries after the constant chatter of her customers; not that she minded talking to them, but after eight solid hours, she needed a break. Krish had told her she was the only person he knew who actually liked cleaning, but she found it therapeutic.

"There," she said to herself as she stood back to admire her handiwork. The salon was sparkling. The floors were clean, the mirrors shone and she could see her reflection in the silver utensil trays.

The only problem was her missing scissors. She still hadn't found them. If they didn't turn up tomorrow, she'd have to rummage through the storeroom cupboard for another pair. She had backups, so it wasn't a train wreck, but they were expensive, and she wanted to find them.

The vintage-style clock on the wall said it was almost nine o'clock. Time to go home.

Daisy glanced out of the shop window. It was still pelting down. The sound of the rain was drowned out by Cavalli, but she could see by the big, wide splatters that it was torrential.

"Darn rain," she muttered. Her car was at home, so it would be a very wet, ten-minute walk back to her cottage, and her umbrella—which had a nasty habit of inverting itself— would offer little protection in this wind.

She locked the front door from the inside and turned off the lights and the radio before walking through to the kitchenette at the back. Suddenly, the rain seemed inordinately loud. Suppressing a shiver, she pulled on her coat and gloves and grabbed her umbrella.

I'm going to get drenched, she thought as she opened the back door and sharp daggers of rain pierced her skin. Squinting, she opened her umbrella and stepped out into the deluge.

Here goes.

She locked the door behind her and then turned around and nearly fell over someone lying about a meter from the doorway. "What the . . . ?"

She bent down, immediately recognizing the hair because she'd styled it herself only that morning. It was Melanie Haverstock, one of her customers! And she was lying in the sodden street with Daisy's missing scissors sticking out of her back.

Connect with

Grab These Cozy Mysteries
from
Kensington Books